DAWN OF DESTINY

DAWN OF DESTINY

A NEW DAWN™ BOOK ONE

AMY HOPKINS

MICHAEL ANDERLE

JIT Beta Readers

John Findlay
Kelly O'Donnell
Paul Westman
Alex Wilson
James Caplan
Larry Omans
Keith Verret
Micky Cocker
Tim Bischoff
Peter Manis

If I missed anyone, please let me know!

Editor

Candy Crum

From Amy

This book is dedicated to my darling children, whose voracious appetites,
destructive mess, lack of logical reasoning and occasional
toilet-training mishaps inspired my take on the remnant.

From Michael

To Family, Friends and
Those Who Love To Read.
May We All Enjoy Grace
To Live The Life We AreCalled.

PROLOGUE

The future is not what we expected.

After our greatest heroes left Earth to carry their justice to the stars, war broke out between those who remained behind. Eventually, the alien technology that once enhanced a select few began to change, infecting the blood of all humans, bringing about an Age of Madness.

But that mutation allowed the survivors to access powers beyond their imaginations...

As society began to rebuild, those who could tame the powers within started calling it by another name.

Magic.

Years passed, and the true history of our world turned to legend. Strange societies formed, each with their own myths and methods to control the power.

But new abilities has led to new evil...and the need for new heroes.

Welcome to the Age of Magic.

C H A P T E R   O N E

Julianne watched the display, her expression unreadable. She didn't react when a small girl, dressed in white, took a shot to the chest. Bright red blossomed on the girl's white robes and she fell, eyes wide open in fear and shock.

Faceless guards with magical weapons shot down mystics without remorse. Julianne watched. The victims tried to fight, evidenced by hands to heads and furious looks of concentration. Still, they fell.

Only when there was no one left to fight back did the illusion finally fade, dissipating into thin air to reveal the solid stone walls of the Mystic Temple. Thunder boomed in the distance, causing more than one spectator to shudder.

This was the third scenario Julianne had sat through tonight. She had returned to the Heights some months ago after helping to free the nearby city, Arcadia, from Adrien, a physical mage turned dictator. Since then, tensions in the Mystic Temple were high.

As a group, mystics were generally peace loving and quite isolated. This was the first time in memory they had involved themselves in the politics of nearby Arcadia. Or, Julianne thought wryly, *she* had involved them. As the strongest among them and their leader, she was the one who had masqueraded as a city guard to help bring down Adrien, and the corrupt nobles who followed him.

"This is our fate, if we do nothing." Jonsen, a mystic of middling power but much ambition, nodded to the small girl that weaved the image he'd projected from his mind. He smirked, confident he'd made a mark on the watchers and convinced them of the danger that lay ahead if they did nothing, if they refused to arm themselves and prepare for war.

He wasn't a warmonger, far from it. Until recently, Julianne would have picked him to side with the pacifists, to push for the laying down of weapons in favor of submission. Still, the preceding months had been tough on all of them, and some of her mystics had undergone similar changes.

Zoe was a master story-crafter, her skill honed through years of practice. Jonsen had used that skill to project his images. The entire hall had watched, mesmerized, as his thoughts took shape through her magic. Zoe, eyes white as she worked her magic, had shown them a picture of the Mystic Temple as it was set upon by Arcadians using the lethal weapons Adrien created before his demise.

While the scene unfolded, Jonsen narrated it. He began with truth, recreating a scene that was etched into the mind of every mystic who had been present the night they had been attacked.

The emissaries from Arcadia had seemed benign at first glance, but it hadn't taken long for one of the mystic guards to slip inside one of the Arcadian's heads. Their leader quickly realized and all hell broke loose. An Arcadian shot a mystic, and Julianne had, with the help of Ezekiel, gone into battle mode.

Jonsen didn't touch on the fact that the Arcadians had been looking for Ezekiel, and Julianne was glad. Even the timidest among them would never turn away someone in need. That night, Julianne and Zeke had shut down the attack, but Jonsen put forth a different version. What would have happened if Julianne and Zeke hadn't been here to protect them?

Carnage, according to the illusions crafted from his story; the annihilation of the mystics and absolute rule by a despicable man for the rest of the nation.

"And that, my fellow mystics, is why we need to begin training at once. Our defenses are low, we have taken peace for granted far too long. The next time we are attacked may be our last." Jonsen slammed one fist into his palm, with a look of righteous determination. "We *must not* allow that to happen!"

Julianne pushed past her migraine to touch the minds around her. Jonsen's confidence was contagious and more than a few minds held whispers of support for his idea. Still, some resisted. Sensing his time to speak was up, Jonsen walked back to sit at his table.

Julianne didn't react when someone leaned close to whisper in her ear. "I have a handful of coins that say Thomas will beat Melanie to the floor."

"Danil, this isn't the time for wagers." Julianne turned to her companion, resisting the urge to roll her eyes. Even during this mess, his tone was light.

Danil smiled, his freckled face turned just a bit too far to the left. When he saw that she'd noticed, he adjusted, using his mind reading ability to compensate for his blindness. "It is *exactly* the time for wagers. Quick… they're both about to stand."

"Melanie," Julianne said quickly, turning back to watch the room.

Thomas stood and Danil smiled, his grin dropping when Melanie saw she was about to be beaten and shot to her feet. She pushed Thomas aside and hurried into the center of the room.

"I request the right to speak," she called out. The angry waves of emotion that boiled from her contradicted the call for peace she was about to make. "And I request the same boon from Zoe that was given to Jonsen."

Zoe sighed and nodded. Julianne briefly touched on the girl's mind.

I've got the energy to spare, Zoe said in Julianne's mind. *And now I'm a few coins richer. Danil lost to both of us.*

Julianne was too far away to see the twinkle in Zoe's eyes but knew it was there. She stifled a snort into her cup.

"I know, not the time. *Especially* with an empty purse," Danil moaned.

"Don't play poor with me, Danil." Julianne gave him a jab with her elbow. "I know how often you lose, and it's not enough to claim poor after one bad bet."

The grin crept back over Danil's face. He was her best friend and a damn good mystic, but his love of games often drove her mad. "True. But I think I'll hold off on any more wagers for now. Too evenly split." He slid back in his chair, letting the dark hair of his fringe flop over his face.

As Melanie took the center of the dining hall, she whispered a word to weave a little magic to make sure all the mystics were attuned to her words. She couldn't directly improve their hearing, but she could make them force their attention on her words.

She stood tall, her dark eyes glittering in the light. Julianne stifled a groan. Melanie brought her as much angst as Danil brought joy.

Bloody woman would argue about the need for dinner if we let her, Julianne mused, the thought shielded from her mind-reading companions.

They'd often butted heads. Though Melanie was one of the senior mystics and the one in charge of their student component, Julianne still outranked her. Of course, Julianne outranked everyone.

Though there seemed to be no animosity in it, Melanie had made it her mission to ensure Julianne had the opportunity to see both sides of *every* argument. She was a professional devil's advocate.

Melanie cleared her throat. "To prepare for war is to invite it," she said, as Zoe's illusion unfolded. The Mystics' Temple, tall and proud as it sat upon the Heights, came into view. "We have survived long by taking a peaceful role, by keeping clear of Irth politics. To show force, to involve ourselves where we should not, is to show we need to be subdued."

The illusion darkened as mystics appeared at every window, pointing weapons, eyes white to show their magic. A horde of soldiers swarmed up the craggy cliffs of the Heights. The panoramic image zoomed into the doors, where mystic fought soldier, and blood was shed.

The mystics were overpowered as the room whispered with mental impressions of fear and discomfort. Julianne stifled a sigh of impatience. She knew where this was heading.

"Do we wish to make ourselves targets? More than that, how many here could live with the burdens you ask us to shoulder?"

The illusion shifted. A soldier, young and vibrant, excited for the chance to defend his people. Pink cheeked and curly haired, he looked up at the foreboding castle and whispered a vow to protect his family and friends back home. His face, shown again, smeared with blood and drained of color, dead.

Julianne's eyes narrowed. Melanie was pushing the whole thing a bit far. Still, she sat quietly, not wanting to interrupt. She would have her chance to speak at the end.

Men fell in battle, some barely more than boys. A mother cried as news of her soldier son's death descended. A mystic, faceless but recognizable in the white robes they wore while on pilgrimage, stood trial. She raised her head and whispered, "Guilty. I plead guilty."

Oh, fuck this, Julianne thought.

Julianne shot to her feet, her chair squawking loudly on the stone floor. The images vanished. Melanie stepped back, her surprise so strong it was likely evident to one who couldn't read minds and emotions.

"What the *hell* do you think I was doing in Arcadia? Stealing from babies? Laying waste to a village of innocents?" Julianne growled, her patience gone.

The mystic leader stepped into the center of the room, waving away Zoe's offer to project images. Though Julianne was technically stronger than the girl in every aspect of mental magic, Zoe had a flair for storytelling that was second to none.

Tonight, however, Julianne wanted to rely on her words, not a half-cocked story that pulled at heartstrings.

"Adrien was a tyrant. He beat the poor and middle class into the ground, then killed them because he could. He restricted magic to the noble born, using it only to grow his own wealth and power. He ignored his duty as a ruler, twisted it for his own evil purposes. His people starved in the streets, or died in his dungeons. They had but a sole source of clean water. One tiny spout for the entire Boulevard, home to the poor. Even nobles weren't immune to his violence."

Julianne turned slowly, meeting the eyes of as many as she could. Her heart raced and her blood boiled at the weak arguments that had been presented. Cowards, all of them.

"Yes," she snapped as faces turned away from her unshielded thought. "*Cowards.* Our powers are a gift, a gift that helped pull us from the age of madness. They're not a right, and if we're not going to use them to help this broken world pull its shit together, we don't deserve them."

"Our magic is—" Melanie began in a wavering voice.

"A responsibility!" Julianne shouted. Blowing out a hard breath, she tempered her voice. "We don't need to become mindless killing machines to protect the weak. We *do* need to stand up for what's right, we can't ignore those who seek to exploit the innocent. We must be the defenders, the protectors of this world. We're not alone. We have Ezekiel and Hannah and others to help, but we can't sit by and let them shoulder this burden alone."

Melanie exuded a sliver of satisfaction at that.

"Yes," Julianne said with a narrow glare at the woman. "It *will* be a burden. We will need to make hard choices, put ourselves in uncomfortable positions. Is that *more* of a burden than letting the world collapse under the likes of Adrien?"

As images of what she'd seen in the previous months flickered through her mind, Julianne finally projected them. Rather than a carefully crafted story, these were disjointed, rough. These were real, things she'd seen, smelled, experienced firsthand.

A child begging on the street, full of helpless desperation. A young man, lying in the gutter. He looked like a drunk turned out to dry, but Julianne's gentle probe had shown him to be beaten almost to death by Adrien's guards.

A moment's work had revealed his crime: arguing over the hefty portion of money he'd been told to hand over to one of Adrien's goons. A woman, crying because her husband had gone to work in Adrien's factory. She hadn't seen him for weeks, and though the weekly paycheck kept coming, she knew in her heart he was dead.

She then showed the men freed from Adrien's sweatshop, starving and weak but still eager to fight, to reclaim their city. A noblewoman, her dress worn and dirty as she taught a small group of children in rags. The ruins of an old building teeming with refugees after the city itself fell. Nobles and poor training together, breaking down the barriers Adrien had forced on them.

She showed them the power of people coming together. The small, war-torn group of refugees, led by the Founder Ezekiel and his apprentice Hannah, had mounted a solid defense against Adrien and given their lives to stop his blood-soaked reign over Arcadia. They, who had nothing, had fought with everything.

Passion ignited Julianne's images in a white-hot flame, flickering out as she regained control of her emotions. She knew she'd accomplished what she needed to. The room buzzed with energy, and the minds she brushed showed new understanding of why she had gone to Arcadia. As if in response to Julianne's storytelling, the storm outside crashed into the Temple. Lightning flashed, drowning the lanterns in the hall with white brilliance.

Melanie's eyes met Julianne's, only for a moment. Then, the other woman dropped her head, submitting to Julianne's experiences and talent. A mischievous spark flared, quickly suppressed. Julianne smiled. The other woman might be the ultimate devil's advocate, but after making her case, she would always bow to the better decision.

The mood of the room settled as Julianne stepped back to her seat, silently rehearsing her proposal to begin training all mystics in the art of self-defense, and to form new classes that would teach those willing to use their magic like warriors.

She was interrupted by another white flash, and the following thunder cracked right on its heels. A spike of anxiety in the room touched Julianne's senses, and she shook her head, knowing the old building would weather the storm.

"It's not the storm," Danil whispered as she sat beside him. Julianne jerked her head up, reaching her mind out to the crowd of mystics in the hall, then further, to the guards. Yes, there it was.

Someone was at the door.

CHAPTER TWO

Who is it, Aldred? Julianne projected into the mind of one of the Temple guards.

I can't tell, came the bewildered mental reply.

Julianne delved into his mind. He was right, whoever was beating the brass knocker was shielded so tight, none of the mystics at the door could penetrate. She reached out herself, probing the slippery mental barrier.

"Stay here." Julianne ran across the hall, pushing past the few mystics who didn't move out of her way first. *And make sure the others do, too,* she added, sending that thought only to Danil.

Danil sent a mental reply that was more a serious nod than words.

"Master," Aldred called as she raced to the entry of the Temple. "Can you sense them?"

She shook her head brusquely and walked up to the door. Aldred already had his hand on the latch, waiting for Julianne's instructions. His heavy frame looked as fit as ever, but grey streaks at his temples reminded her that time passed in the mountains just as quickly as everywhere else.

William, the second guard on duty, stepped aside to let her through, ducking his sandy haired head at the Mystic Master.

Who is there? She sent the words directly at the shielded mind, projecting the thought as loudly as she could. Even shielded, a mystic would hear it.

Greetings, Julianne. Please, open the door.

Julianne clamped down her mental shields, furious that she hadn't thought to do so earlier.

Donna? William sent the name with a feeling of shock.

"Who the hell is Donna?" Julianne hissed.

"An old friend. She and two others went on pilgrimage… oh, years before Selah…" He stopped before saying the word *died*, but Julianne still heard him speak it in his mind. The death of the former Master marked much time in the Heights for all of them. "Well, I haven't heard from her since."

"Can she be trusted?" Julianne asked, brushing aside a mental probe sent by the visitors.

"Yes," William said, "assuming she's not changed greatly. Selah thought highly of her." He added the last part as an afterthought.

Julianne still hesitated.

Please, Donna sent. *The storm will wash us off the mountain if we do not find shelter immediately.*

The thread of fear in the woman's thought stabbed at Julianne. She couldn't allow people—her people—to die outside the gates that were supposed to keep them safe. She instructed William and Aldred to open the heavy wooden doors, even as she forced away a memory of a guard almost dying on the very floor below her feet.

That was different, she told herself. And it was. When Adrien sent his soldiers looking for Ezekiel, she'd immediately known to be on guard. An over eager blast from one of the soldiers had hit one of her men. Ezekiel had not only taken out the attackers with Julianne's help, he'd healed the wounded mystic guardsman and likely saved his life.

They were Arcadians, though. Not mystics.

The two guards lifted the bar that held the doors shut. Wind slammed them open, almost knocking Aldred flat on his ass as six robed figures hurried in. With their help, it only took a moment for the two guards to recover and latch the doors shut again while Julianne examined their visitors.

"William!" A tall woman pushed back her hood, revealing a mess of red curls threaded with silver. She leaned in to give William a breathy kiss on the cheek and his face reddened. A brief memory flickered in Williams' mind, and Julianne saw that they were more than just 'old friends'.

Rather than probe, Julianne turned her attention to the others. They wore matching robes of sky blue silk, trimmed with silver thread. A symbol was embroidered onto the chest and back, one of the sun cresting over two hills. Something about it made Julianne's stomach twist, though she made sure to cloak that reaction tightly behind her mental shield.

"You must be Selah's replacement? I'd heard he'd left the Temple to a *girl*, but I hadn't expected one quite so young." Donna ran her eyes up and down Julianne's small frame, her face neutral.

"I am Julianne, the Master of the mystics," Julianne conceded, ignoring the subtle jab at her age.

"Well, we are glad to have made it here. The hike up that mountain was almost as bad as trekking through the Madlands. I expect the evening meal is still at the same time?" Donna asked before sweeping past Julianne in the direction of the great hall. "Ensure your people have enough for guests."

Bristling at Donna's attitude, Julianne followed, nodding for the two guards to remain behind. Five robed figures trailed behind, silent, as they made their way through the Temple.

Donna strode into the hall with confidence, bestowing smiles and greetings on those she recognized, warmly introducing herself to those she didn't. As her followers pushed back their hoods, Julianne caught more flickers of recognition from nearby mystics.

She delved into those minds and quickly learned the entire group were mystics from the Heights, trained when Selah was at his peak. They had all set off for various reasons; some to find new talents, others to learn and stretch their minds, and one because he was just plain restless.

None had been heard from in at least five years. All were well-liked members of the community, with friends and some even family, but they'd all just… faded away. That in itself wasn't uncommon. Pilgrimages could last decades. The rustles of worries and discomfort were for another reason.

Julianne tried again to penetrate their shields, this time going for a quiet, older man instead of Donna. Nothing. Her attempts met an impenetrable wall, slipping aside as though the old man's mind was made of glass. Julianne muttered a curse under her breath.

"Steady." Danil appeared beside her, taking her arm and leading her back to her spot at the table. "There might be a reasonable explanation for this. Maybe they're launching a new fashion line, and want you to model for them."

"If they think they're going to cause trouble here, they're in for a shock," Julianne grumbled. She gave up trying to use her magic on them, instead saving her energy in case it was needed later.

"It's not like no one has ever been able to shield from you before." Danil hesitated. "Have they?"

Julianne eyed him, raising her own shields to cover a memory of a man who'd done just that. He wasn't even a mystic! He hadn't just blocked her from his mind, he'd caught her heart, too. Julianne breathed deeply to keep her cheeks from coloring as thoughts of Marcus, the Arcadian guard, rushed through her mind.

"Friends! Thank you for welcoming us back into our home."

Donna's voice carried over the pockets of conversation in the room.

Julianne hadn't noticed the noise when she came in, but a quick brush against the closest minds showed every one of them locked down. The mystics were shielding so tightly it was making mind-to-mind conversations difficult, and the normally subdued dining hall was full of noise. If Julianne had a headache before, now it was bordering on a migraine.

"The Temple welcomes all who come in peace." Julianne let the words drop with all the weight they deserved.

Had they come in peace?

Donna smiled. It did not reach her eyes. "We come not only in peace, but offering gifts. We have heard of your efforts, dear Julianne, and have come to join you in your fight. You will find our resources run deep."

"Our fight? What fight?" Samantha, a middle-aged mystic called out. "Arcadia is safe, there's no fighting left to be done."

A space cleared, leaving Donna alone in the middle of the room.

"Your fight against the Arcadians is not over, far from it." Donna gave Julianne a small bow. "We fight not just the people, but the depravity of mankind, and the failings of those who are not blessed to know the minds of others."

Donna turned to her audience. "For it is our power to read minds that allows us to rise above. Only we, who can truly experience empathy and walk in the shoes of another, are immune to the greed and treachery, the utter selfishness of the human race. Only we are fit to guide the people into a bright new future."

"Not wearing that color blue with that hair, you're not," Danil mumbled.

Julianne raised an eyebrow. "What the hell are you saying? That we're some kind of superior race?"

Donna shrugged, as if to ask what else she could possibly be saying.

"You know what?" Julianne stalked around the table and went to stand toe to toe with the other woman. "That shit sounds awfully similar to what Adrien thought. I assume you know who he was?"

Donna shook her head. "My knowledge of the recent battles is scant. The condition of mankind, however, is something I am well versed in."

"He was a magic user who thought he was better than others. He thought his way was the right way, and damned anyone who disagreed. He trod on the weak and helpless, ground them into the dirt while climbing to a higher station." Julianne paused, narrowing her eyes. "And he's dead. I helped to take him down, because that kind of behavior is exactly what our magic is supposed to stand against."

"Of course!" Donna smiled. "What a horrible man. We would never align ourselves with someone like that, and indeed, it was those exploits that brought us here. But please, we have had a long journey. Perhaps this would be best discussed in the morning?"

Julianne carefully shielded her next thoughts. The pretty woman looked as though she'd stepped out of a manor house, not undertaken a long journey. The few mystics in the room whose feelings could still be read emitted blatant distrust. Julianne was inclined to agree with them.

"Very well," she said. "Morning. The guards will escort you to your rooms and refreshments will be delivered soon after. Be warned, we rise early."

"We always have," Donna said with a saccharin smile. "I'm sure by then we will have convinced you of the value of an alliance. Together, the New Dawn and the mystics of the Heights will rule the world!"

She took the arm of the first guard to enter and swept away like a lady in her own manor house.

CHAPTER THREE

Good grief, the girl is strong. Reva sent the thought to Donna's mind directly, hiding the exchange from the other members of the New Dawn, and from the mystic guard escorting them to one of the visitors rooms. *If she keeps pushing like that tomorrow, I don't know if we can hold her off.*

Don't be ridiculous, Donna sent, her thoughts laced with irritated exhaustion. Julianne was strong, but they had the advantage... for now. *All we have to do is keep that shield up. We've practiced this. She doesn't know our methods, or our strength.*

Reva bit her tongue. Their 'strength' was nothing but a parlour trick that enhanced their mental shield, and it relied on everyone in their group staying strong. Sure, they'd had a ton of practice... but never against anything like Julianne.

Stop it, Donna warned. *We were sent here to do one of two things. As long as our shield stays up, we are safe.*

And if it doesn't? Reva thought timidly.

Back in the dining hall, the door banged shut, leaving the room in silence. One by one, minds unshielded to reveal an overwhelming current of unrest.

A thread of calm wove through, and Julianne traced it back to Margit, one of the older mystics present. Grateful for the prompt, Julianne copied the soothing waves, touching the minds of the most afraid first and moving on when that person had calmed. Despite Donna's absence, Julianne kept her thoughts locked down.

"You're all worried," she called out when the room had begun to settle. "Despite our recent discussions, I know we all feel the same way. People are not chattel. Everyone, no matter their status or whether they can use magic, deserves a good and fair life."

"With wine and women and laughter," Danil added with a grin. The room ignored him.

"We have disagreed on my choice to involve myself in the fight with Adrien, and I respect that. I know that even those who wish I'd stayed behind are just worried about our own safety, that none of you think another human should be controlled or enslaved just because of how or where they were born."

"She didn't mean it, though. Did she?" A younger man looked around for confirmation from his peers. "She doesn't want to rule the world, just..." He trailed off at the glowering faces beside him.

"What do we do? Surely, you don't agree with her?" a voice called out.

"Nor do we want to start a war with another faction of our own!" came a reply. Julianne recognized both as the speakers from earlier in the night.

"Or submit ourselves to such awful taste in robes." Danil's gripe caused a ripple of light chuckles in the nearby crowd this time. Leaning back, a satisfied smile on his face.

"Right now, we will do nothing," Julianne assured them. "We will let Donna and her people plead their case in the morning. Maybe it's just a case of mixed messages. Then, a meeting of the seniors will be called, and we will figure this out together." She ran her eyes over the pale faces before her. "I promise, nothing will be decided by one person alone. Not this time."

Tentatively, she reached out to gauge the mood in the room. She was surprised to feel, amongst the worry and fear, a sense of pride and security at her words. They respected her as their Master, she knew that. But proud of her? She had to fight to keep the color from her cheeks and was glad she'd left her mental shield up when the guests had left the room.

"Go and rest. Our visitors will be watched through the night and in the morning, we will see what they have to say."

Julianne sat back down and took a long swallow of elixir, then pressed the chilled glass to her forehead.

J, you need to do something about those headaches, Danil sent.

What? The sudden mental intrusion took Julianne by surprise. *It's fine, just a little worried about the newcomers.*

He's right, Margit chimed in. *You're overexerting yourself. You might be stronger than the rest of us, but that doesn't mean you're smarter. Listen to Danil. He at least has a brain in his head.*

Me? Brain? I reject that accusation, Danil retorted.

Margit was a mother figure to many of those who'd come to the mystics at a young age. Though her talent for magic was average, her sharp mind and firm manner made her perfect to address the needs of the children.

She helped with their schooling a little, teaching them history and politics, but also made sure their teeth were clean and clothes tidy, that they took to their beds at a reasonable time and made them up in the morning.

I'm fine. Julianne sent the words with confidence. She had been pushing herself harder, but she was getting stronger for it. A little pain was worth the extra power, and Julianne had a feeling she'd need every bit of it.

Very well, Margit sent. The door to the great hall creaked shut as the last of the mystics left, leaving Julianne with Danil, Margit, and Zoe. "But don't come crying to me when you burn yourself out." She enveloped Julianne in a tight hug.

"I won't, Margit." Julianne gestured for Zoe to come sit at the head table with them. "Do you think I did the right thing?"

Margit raised an eyebrow. "You want to know what I'd have done?"

Julianne laughed. "Turned them over your knee and spanked them, probably. They should be safe enough, but what about tomorrow? I can't just let them run around the countryside if they truly do pose a threat, but how can I stop them without alienating half the people who live here? If I start imprisoning people on a gut feeling, I'm no better than Adrien."

"This threat is a lot closer to home than Adrien was," Margit pushed. "Those tree-hugging peace lovers will realize their options resemble a choice between a used chamber pot and a bucket of shit. They'll come around."

Zoe's thoughts were loud enough that she didn't need to voice them.

"No, Zoe," Julianne said before anyone else could speak. "I won't delay my trip. In fact, this makes it even more pressing."

In two days, Julianne had planned a private pilgrimage. An old mystic named Artemis, one with an odd manner and not much talent but an obsession with learning, was recently seen across the Madlands. Though travelers from that direction were rare, the rumor had instantly piqued Julianne's curiosity.

"You're heading off on nothing but a rumor, and leaving us alone with that cult stalking the Heights?" Zoe asked.

"It's more than just a story. I've spoken to four people who remember him—Margit included." Julianne nodded at the older woman.

"I do remember Artemis, but damned if I know how you think you'll find him. The man never was happy amongst people and could go days without being seen even here in the Heights." Margit's face softened fondly as she remembered him.

Zoe screwed up her face. "I still don't think it's safe. Not for you, or for us. Who knows how many more of those New Dawn people are roaming the countryside?"

"Zoe's right. We need to discuss where to go from here." Danil spoke slowly, but Julianne could feel his mind racing. "Tomorrow's agenda, other than this mess?" he asked, knowing the others would have read his thoughts.

Danil wanted to begin training the younger residents basic self-defense skills and to re-examine the security measures put in place since the events of Arcadia.

Julianne nodded. "I think we need to discuss it, at least. I don't want to scare anyone more than we already have." With a deep sigh, she stood. "I miss the days when all we did was talk philosophy and drink elixir. I need sleep first, though." Julianne stood and the others followed.

"My dear girl, would you mind helping me up to my room? These old joints need more than a bit of elixir to loosen them." Julianne nodded in response to Margit's request. Margit waved away Danil's offer to help, then eyed the cup still loosely grasped in his hand. "You going to drink that?"

He snorted a laugh and handed it over. Margit leaned on Julianne's arm, holding her cup out so it didn't spill as they left the room.

"I expect you've led me away to offer some kind of sage advice?" Julianne murmured as they reached the stairs.

"Advice? I just wanted help so I didn't spill my drink." As if to emphasize her point, she stopped and took a mouthful. "Sometimes I wish this stuff had a little more kick, like that mead they drink down at Craigston."

"If it did, the entire mystic community would be stumbling around drunk every day," Julianne said wryly. The elixir had been crafted to soothe the mind of magic users without the side effects of alcohol.

"Most of those fools wouldn't know the difference." Margit handed Julianne the now empty glass, dropping the girl's arm in favor of the stair railing. "Of course, if you *want* advice, I'm happy to oblige."

Julianne rolled her eyes and dropped Margit's arm.

"Last time you gave me advice, it was to find a hot young stud to train up as my assistant. What was it you said? 'Why do it yourself when someone can do it for you, all while they're doing you, too?'"

The woman smiled and paused at the top of the stairs. "You are the master of this domain, Julianne. Selah left you in charge for a reason."

"Because I was the strongest," Julianne said, knowing it was her magical strength that had gained her the position.

"Oh, don't be *ridiculous*. You think he'd have left an idiot in charge, or a warmonger?"

Julianne had to admit it as unlikely. Selah had been an idealist, and a kind man. He had to have some level of trust in Julianne above her technical ability to give her the title of Master when he was gone.

"Selah always knew you'd be our next leader. Not because you're strong, but because you kicked a rearick boy in the nuts for threatening his girl." The old woman paused, watching Julianne's reaction. "Oh, I see you remember that."

"Margit, that was a terrible thing to do! I couldn't face Selah for days after."

"And when you did?" Margit waited expectantly.

Julianne sighed. "He told me my spirit would get me in trouble, but he couldn't fault my reasoning."

"You are kind, girl." Margit reached a hand up to touch Julianne's cheek. "And you are strong, and fierce, and you will keep our people safe. Not just our skins, worthless as they are, but our souls. You'll lead us into a fight we were too scared to start, one we need to start if we are to live with ourselves when the sun goes down."

Tears pricked at Julianne's eyes as she hugged Margit good-night. "Thank you," she whispered to the old woman. *And thank you, too, Selah,* she thought, wishing she could tell her mentor one last time.

CHAPTER FOUR

The next morning, Julianne sat at her place at the head table, mind tightly shielded as she watched the newcomers prepare to speak.

"I imagine the tradition of storytelling still persists?" Donna asked, bowing to Julianne.

Julianne nodded slowly. "Naturally."

"Then with your permission, I will take the floor."

Donna stepped forward into the center of the room, and Julianne settled in to watch the display.

Donna waited patiently until the room was silent before launching into her story. She projected her own images, eyes white as her magic worked.

"The New Dawn have isolated ourselves too long, hoping for the day we can rise to take our true place. Imagine our joy when news came that a girl had toppled the weak leaders of our kind. We knew she would be the one to lead us into a new dawn."

An image formed of a girl. She had no face but wore Julianne's long, chestnut hair. She stood tall, sunlight radiating behind her as she raised a staff and struck down a frail old man. Sickened fury clouded Julianne's vision, almost choking her magic off and shattering her mental shield. She gritted her teeth and forced slow breaths as she regained control. A hand touched her arm and she gave Danil a grateful look.

"This girl seized her destiny, and pushed on to defeat the bigger threat—the evil of mankind. She stormed the gates of Arcadia, wiping the area clean of the vermin, smiting those who lived in squalor, stealing and gambling their lives away."

Julianne seethed silently as the illusion showed the girl storming the city gates, waving the golden staff over people who cowered at her feet. Magic flowed from her in shimmering waves, and the people on the ground turned their eyes up. Fear and anger on their faces melted, replaced with the kind of vacant adoration that could only come from strong mental magic.

"She fought on, defeating those with inferior magic." Now, it showed fireballs flying towards the girl, dissipating as they got close. "She cut out the rot within the city, right through its very core. When she finished, those who lacked the empathy and wisdom of the mystics were cowed.

"She mastered them, drove them to their knees. Then, she taught them to love. This love drowned the base urges they were cursed with, urges that can only be conquered by those who can read the thoughts of another."

The girl in the image sat, a gilded throne appearing beneath her as she did. Swarms of people clustered around her feet, kissing them and staring up with love-struck eyes. The girl ignored them, staring ahead as the image swooped out to show her stare resting on the tree-covered lands around her.

"We, the New Dawn, wish to help. We will provide trained fighters to stand by your side as you bring the mystics of Irth into their rightful place, as we have in our own lands."

Narrowing back into the girl again, this time the image had changed. Behind her stood five robed figures, faces dark inside their hoods. Instead of a staff of gnarled wood, she now held one of iron, topped with the strange sun symbol the New Dawn wore on their cuffs.

That was enough. Julianne shot to her feet, heedless of Danil's warning tug on her arm. "You said a ruler can't be fit unless they can read minds, feel true empathy. How in the hell can you walk past the pity and desperation in the streets of Arcadia and think those poor people need to be beaten and flogged more than they have? And then what? You *mind control* them into loving you?"

"You know," Danil said, standing beside her. "If you can't find a man the usual way, it's easier to drop a bit of coin. I know of a brothel in—"

"Poor people?" Donna ignored Danil, cutting him off. "I have seen inside their minds, just as you have, *great leader*." She spat the words like venom. "Those people lie and cheat and steal from their betters. Their *betters* kill and rape and abuse the power they were given by the gods. How—"

"The gods?" Julianne barked a laugh. "What gods? The Bitch and the Bastard are long gone, and any power they left should be employed to protect. Not enslave. We know our history—If Bethany Anne came back and saw what you're planning, she'd kick your ass. So will I, if you don't back down."

Julianne lashed out with her mental power, anger fueling her usually calm casting. Rather than slip away, this time it pierced the protective barrier just long enough for Julianne to glimpse inside the other woman's mind.

Darkness. Glory. A mind that was so bent, so warped, that Julianne couldn't make sense of it before she was shoved out. Despite that, Julianne saw what she needed to. Donna's mind had never been pure, but it had been twisted by a mystic, and a strong one at that.

"Out." Everyone in the room jumped at Julianne's sudden command. "Everyone, get the *hell* out." This time, she shoved a thread of compulsion through the words.

Her eyes scanned the room, pushing the command to

everyone but the woman who stood alone in the center of the room. As people hurried to leave Julianne and Donna alone, facing each other across the heavy wooden table, minds brushed each other. Julianne reached out with her mental magic and grabbed at three familiar thought patterns.

Danil was easiest to link to, due to their close relationship. Zoe, too, quickly formed a mind bond with the mystic leader. Margit was harder. Julianne probed the upper levels until she found the sleeping woman and mentally jostled her awake. After a moment's reflection, she also reached out to pull Aldred in.

Watch, Julianne sent, then released her magic. The others stayed in her mind, safe behind Julianne's protective shields as they watched through her eyes.

CHAPTER FIVE

The hall door slammed shut and Julianne looked up, eyes blazing with anger.

Donna opened her mouth to speak, but Julianne cut her off.

"Drop the bullshit. You're not doing this for the benefit of society's dregs; you're doing it for your leader. What kind of hold does he have over you?"

"He showed me the truth. These people aren't worth saving, but they can be of use." Donna smirked, but a slight hesitance in her expression showed Julianne she'd thrown her off balance. "Don't be so precious, warrior-queen. I doubt your motives for going into battle were half as pure as you claim."

Julianne bared her teeth in anger. "Let me make this perfectly clear. You and your kind are not welcome here. Not in the Heights, not in Arcadia, not on this side of the Madlands."

In a flash of anger, she lashed out at Donna's shields again, and again, she pushed past. A figure formed before her eyes. A man, strong and beautiful, along with a feeling of pure desire. Not lust, but a desire to please, to perform like a marionette on strings for the man.

"*My* kind?" Donna's voice was deadly smooth, but the interruption was jarring.

Julianne blinked, then focused back on the conversation. "The mystics of the Heights fight for equality for all. Anyone who thinks they can put themselves above the common people and use them, restrict their magic or work them like slaves, or just pretend they're more entitled, is wrong. We'll fight to the death to prevent that." A slight smile formed on her lips. "And we'll win."

Donna took a step back. "You don't know who you're dealing with, *child.*"

"Maybe not who, but what. Your leader, the one you adore? *Think*, Donna!" Despite the woman's vile attitude, Julianne's heart twisted with pity. "He's got your head twisted so far backwards you can't tell up from down. You don't think he's manipulated you the same way you think we should do to others?" Julianne fell silent, letting her opponent think on her words.

Donna didn't take the chance. "Fool girl! I joined Rogan because he was *right*. He sees so much more than the rest of us, and he will lead us to glory! By casting us out and rejecting his support, you become our enemy. Think hard before making your people a target."

"Get out. I won't throw you off the mountain in this storm, but if you aren't gone by daylight I may reconsider." Julianne waited until Donna was almost at the door before adding, "And if you think *my people* will make an easy target, you'd best think twice."

Donna didn't pause, ignoring the guards that flanked her and her hooded followers as they left.

Make sure they're well and truly gone, will you? Julianne sent to Aldred. She jumped into his head and quickly saw he had the full contingent of guards on duty and alert for problems.

Will do, Master, he replied as the mystics of the Heights filed quietly back in to finish their breakfast.

"After breakfast, would the senior members join me in my office?" Julianne called. Margit, Danil, and the three other mystics in question all sent their agreement, and Julianne sat down to eat.

Though her appetite was gone, she reached for some ham and a slice of thick, buttered bread, adding some sweet cherries to her plate as an afterthought. She tried to tune out the whispers and thoughts that drifted by, concentrating instead on her meal.

A young boy and two older girls approached the head table. "Uhh, Master?" Bettina, the oldest, was the first to speak. "Mattie and Birn were just wondering… are we to train in battle magic now?"

"It's just, the younger ones are worried," Mattie asked. Julianne didn't point out he was one of the youngest in the Heights.

"Everything will be fine," she said. "Your teachers and I will decide what happens and yes, your training in the mental disciplines may change. It won't be battle magic, though."

Mattie's eyes dropped and his lips twisted into a childish pout. Bettina nudged him and whispered, "Told you so," as they returned to their seats.

"Little runts are always worried," Danil said through a mouthful of food and a grin. "It's not your fault."

Julianne swallowed her bread. "It doesn't matter whose fault it is. I'm the one responsible for them, and they're scared."

"Bullshit, you're teaching them resilience." Danil shrugged. "And anyway, it is what it is. No point stressing over things out of your control. Best to focus on what you can change and do that… or something like that." Danil frowned as if trying to remember the words Julianne had said to him, and to others, a thousand times over.

"Shut up." Julianne threw a corner of bread at him, closing her eyes so Danil couldn't use her own sight to duck. When he let out a bark of surprise, she opened them to see it had landed in his cup, splashing elixir over his shirt. "Serves you right," she giggled.

Danil made a halfhearted attempt to return the volley, but miscalculated and sent it flying at Bevan, a cranky old mystic who had no tolerance for childish behavior. Of course, that made Julianne laugh even harder, and when Bevan stood to frown over the two of them, she slipped back in her seat clutching her ribs.

As was often the case in a room full of mind readers, her laughter became contagious. Before long, the entire room was happy and relaxed, the events from earlier all but forgotten.

"See?" Danil said with a smile. "Doesn't take long for this lot to recover. It wouldn't be like that if they didn't trust you, J."

Julianne reached over to squeeze his hand gratefully while she watched the mystics' earlier anxiety melt away. Then, with a sigh, she pushed her plate away. "I guess I better get ready for this meeting. Are you coming up now?"

"Sure." Danil rose and took her arm. In a room full of people, Danil could use multiple sets of eyes to 'see' his way around from different angles. The fewer the people, the harder it was for him to judge distance, and the chance that someone was looking just where he needed them to was much lower.

Julianne felt his familiar spike of alertness as the door closed behind them, and he was reduced to using her set of eyes. Still, she didn't bother to change her actions. Danil had lived in the Heights as long as she had and knew every nook and cranny like the back of his hand. Probably better, in fact.

"What time are you headed out?" he asked as they walked.

"Early. Before breakfast, though I don't think I'll make it out before sunup." Julianne shot him a sideways glance. "Why are you shielding me?" she asked. Danil had, at some point after they left the dining hall, locked her out of his head.

"What? Oh, it's just left over from last night I suppose." He dropped the shield, but a section of his mind still remained clouded. Julianne didn't ask him about it. It was common for those at the Heights to guard small parts of their mind, usually to prevent awkwardness or to shield impolite thoughts.

Danil often had a little corner of his mind kept secret, and Julianne had long had the suspicion that he was hiding feelings for her. She knew many of the others suspected so. So far, he hadn't mentioned it and neither had she.

"How do you think the others will want to deal with this?" Julianne asked him, trying to push away her nerves.

"The usual way." He looked at her and, when she shot back a quizzical glance, explained. "They'll throw up suggestions, argue about them, then wait for you to decide. They'll offer a little token resistance to assert their value to the conversation, and walk away relieved that they didn't have to have the final say."

"And you?" Julianne asked.

"I will, as always, offer sage advice and eternal wisdom. Those present shall quake at my valuable insight and lament their puny attempts to compete with my greatness." He bowed, almost tripping on the top step as he did so.

"Oh, for goodness sake, be careful!" Julianne admonished. "The last thing I need is for you to break your neck."

"Because you can't live without my sharp wit and clever ideas?" he asked with a wink.

"Because without the comic relief and constant bullshit you provide, I'd bore myself to death."

They were both laughing as they entered Julianne's office. She waved Danil to one of the seats as she poured him a cup of elixir, then ducked next door to drag a few more chairs into the room. She was shortly joined by Gunther, the head guard.

Quickly reading his hesitant request, Julianne nodded. "Yes, we will need you at our meeting. Thank you." Gunther was a godsend to Julianne, taking her promotion to Master in stride and never questioning her decisions in public, yet forthright enough to let her know if there was a better way.

Footsteps in the hall signaled the arrival of the others, and

Julianne closed her eyes. She sucked a breath in through her nose and slowly released it, taking that brief moment to find her center.

"Welcome Charles, Melanie, and Jonsen. Shall we begin?"

CHAPTER SIX

"I'd like to begin by saying that any objection I had to you leaving for Arcadia no longer exists." Jonsen jumped in to speak before the others could even sit down. "What you've shown us since you've been back made me realize I hadn't grasped the situation at all. In regard to the current situation… well, I'll probably take your lead, Master."

Julianne's heart melted. Jonsen had been the loudest voice against her leaving and the most chastened when she returned. "Thank you, Jonsen."

"I wouldn't go that far myself," Charles said as he lowered himself into a chair, which creaked under his impressive weight. "But I do think many of us geriatrics have shut ourselves in for too long. I admit you have more expertise on current world matters, but damned if I'll let you start arming my students before it's necessary."

"It's long past necessary," Danil said. "Did you hear what that woman said? And I'm twice as worried by the fact that not one— not *one* of us—could make it past her mental shield except Julianne."

"You what? I must have missed that, what did you see?" Charles asked.

"Not much," Julianne admitted. "Enough to know she's under the sway of a very powerful mystic. Her mind is warped. Though I think the contempt she felt was real enough, there's someone more powerful standing behind her."

"Aldred said somewhat the same, Master." Gunther nodded respectfully. "Seems he knew that Donna woman before she left. Said the girl he knew wouldn't break the Temple tenets like that, not if the world turned over."

"Surely," Melanie said, "the best thing we can do is to bunker down, close our doors and lay low."

"And if another band of pilgrims knocks on our door?" Gunther asked. "How will we know if they're regular mystics returning from pilgrimage, or a bunch of crazies?"

Melanie shrugged.

"You can't mean to turn away our own people," Julianne gasped. "Donna and her companions are mystics, remember? They're our people. Our own! We can't turn away every journeyman who comes back seeking refuge. Even if we had the numbers to sustain ourselves, I wouldn't permit it."

Melanie grimaced. "Fair enough. I didn't know any of her lot personally, I just can't fathom any of *our* people speaking like she did." She gave a slight shudder at the memory of Donna's words.

"Danil has a proposal." Julianne gestured to him to present it. She didn't mention it was one he'd been working on since she'd left for Arcadia so many months ago.

Danil explained that he wanted the few mystics who had trained themselves in battle magic to pass that knowledge on to all of the teachers, who would then filter it down to the students. As it stood, only the guards and a small handful of others knew offensive magic techniques.

"I still don't think the younger initiates should be exposed to such things," Melanie snapped. She folded her arms, her stance mimicking the resistance in her mind.

"Melanie, they just saw a madwoman plotting the enslavement and demise of non-magicals!" Danil sat back in his seat, stretching his arms over his head. "And they all heard about the incident of the Capitol Guards infiltration while Ezekiel was here. I get the feeling if we don't do *something* to get them involved, they'll take it into their own hands. Don't you remember what it's like at that age?"

All eyes turned to him, no doubt remembering what *he* was like at that age.

"Melanie is right," Julianne said. The other woman's plea to keep the children out of the battle training had made Julianne think of the children who'd come to her at dinner. "The children can't be expected to bear this burden, nor should they be saddled with the weight of it. We will adjust the junior teaching programs to introduce effective mental blocking and simple disguises a little earlier, but nothing more. Are we all in agreement?"

All heads nodded, even Danil's. It was rare he'd come up against Julianne, even when she contradicted him. Though it often grated on her, she welcomed it now.

"I can double roster my lot so they have a session at the gates, and a session of passing on what they know." Gunther pursed his lips, thinking. "I figure we can run that for at least a couple weeks before they start to grumble. If you're willing to lend us some bodies to ease the workload once we've got a few trained up, we'll have half the Temple up to scratch in under a month."

"That's another pressing issue, Master," Charles said. "When Gunther says, 'half the Temple', that only makes about one hundred and forty people. Adrien might be gone, but we still only have twenty-two initiates and most of those are almost ready to graduate. If we don't replenish our numbers soon, we may find the greater problem we face lies within our own walls."

Heaving a sigh, Julianne leaned back. *That* was a problem

she'd been avoiding. The once teeming Temple was now full of dusty, unused rooms, and the school wing had been reduced to a single class.

"One thing at a time," she said. "We deal with this threat first, or at least evaluate it. I don't want anyone off galivanting through Arcadia alone with these nutters running loose. As soon as it's deemed safe, we'll start sending out search groups, like we used to. No one who's not trained in battle magic, though."

Melanie sat up and opened her mouth, but Julianne cut her off. "No, Melanie, I won't force anyone to learn it. I can't really force anyone to stay in the Temple, either, but I will stress it's highly recommended at this time."

"What about Arcadia?" Danil asked. "Surely, we need to send a message to them. Perhaps a rearick?"

"I can do that on my way to the Madlands," Julianne said. "I leave tomorrow."

Silence fell for a heartbeat. Then, the protests erupted.

Julianne waved them down. "I'll be perfectly safe, and you will function perfectly well without me. I'm far overdue for a pilgrimage of my own." She turned to face Jonsen. "No, Arcadia was *not* a pilgrimage, it was a rescue mission. I didn't have a damned moment to myself that whole time, and I'm aching for some solitude."

Danil's emotions prickled behind her, but he quickly suppressed them. Julianne assumed it was just worry for her safety.

"I've tried to convince her to stay. Believe me, she's stubborn as a *damned* mule." Danil ducked the hand that almost swatted his ear. "You're prettier than one, though." He ducked the next blow, too.

"She's right," Charles said. "The Temple will function without her, however unwilling we may be to do so. Julianne has made considerable headway in making sure we can stand on our own feet after the mess she had to deal with when Selah died."

Julianne winced. "I wouldn't call it a mess, Charles. It was just a bit… disorganized, is all."

Charles snorted. "That's the understatement of the year. It took you months just to sort out his papers. No, dear, no fault of yours. The man was a pack rat, and we do appreciate the changes you've made. Besides, we survived just fine during your trip to Arcadia. Well, most of us. Those that weren't moping about the halls and pining for your company."

Julianne pointedly ignored the bright red flush creeping up Danil's face. "Thank you, Charles. Now, do we have anything else to address?"

"How long will you be gone?" Melanie asked. "What do we do if that lot come back?"

Julianne shrugged. "What we normally do, I guess. We pull back to the safety of the Temple and close our doors until we think of something better. I don't like it, but I also don't want anyone starting a war with these people until I can find out more about them."

Melanie's eyes narrowed. "You're going to try and find them, aren't you?"

"Not exactly," Julianne said. "But by chance, I'm headed in the direction they came from. If I happen to ferret out some information, all the better. My main mission hasn't changed, though. I want to find Artemis, see if I can coax him back to the Heights for a bit. What little work he left behind showed him to be an expert on battle magic, and he may know more about the exact threat we're up against if he's in the same region."

Melanie nodded. "Can't say I envy your position, Julianne. I appreciate your decision regarding the young ones. Now, I imagine we all have a lot to organize before our Master's departure. I shall see you all at dinner."

With that, the meeting was over.

Butterflies danced in Julianne's stomach as she contemplated the journey ahead, and the possible danger she was leaving behind. In her heart, she knew she couldn't delay this trip. No magic could foretell the future, but Julianne had something better than magic in that respect: common sense.

She needed Artemis and damned if she wouldn't go get him, even if she had to drag him back by the toenails.

CHAPTER SEVEN

Julianne spent the rest of the day in a frenzy of preparation. There were schedules to be altered, to reduce the impact of her absence. A pile of paperwork was set aside for 'later' and wouldn't wait until she got back. Bags needed packing, horses looked over, and money counted.

Though Julianne intended to travel light, she would still need clothes, a bedroll, food, water, maps, papers, and a jumble of other necessary items. She'd also need at least one nice robe and the required items to make herself presentable for her brief visit to Arcadia.

"Do I really need six pairs of socks?" she asked Margit, who was helping her pack.

"Have you forgotten what it's like to walk in wet ones, or how long it takes wool to dry?" Margit shook her head and stuffed the extra pairs in Julianne's pack.

Julianne's previous forays into Irth has mostly involved traveling village to village, with no more than a night or two spent sleeping on the road between inns. A trip across the Madlands would take longer, though, and there would be no safe haven or clean bed to sleep in.

Margit dropped a gold belt into her bag. Julianne plucked it out.

"You're being ridiculous." Margit shook her head and threw the belt back in. "You can't go out into the world, representing the Temple while looking like a hobo!"

"Margit, do you think I'm crazy?"

"I think you're devoid of any sense of style." Margit clicked her tongue, tying up the bag's strings and setting it on the floor next to the bed. She smoothed out the blanket and sat, close enough to put an arm around the younger woman. "I wouldn't like you much if I didn't. But this journey? I think you're doing the right thing."

"You knew Artemis best. What should I expect?"

"A fight." Margit removed her arm and turned to look Julianne in the eyes. "You have to remember, Jules. He's not like us. He's… different. Don't appeal to his better nature, and don't think for a moment you can guilt him into coming back for the good of the people. He doesn't give a *damn* about the people."

A sliver of worry snuck through Julianne's bones. "Margit… you don't think—"

"That he's the leader of the New Dawn? Hah!" Margit slapped her knee, laughing. "That old codger would jump off a cliff before he took charge of an apprentice, let alone a gaggle of moon-eyed cows like that. No, he's different, but in a way I can't even explain."

"Then how the hell am I supposed to get him to come back with me?" Julianne pulled at a loose blanket thread, trying to wrap her head around this strange man she'd never met.

"Make it a puzzle. A challenge, if you will. Julianne, where your drive comes from protecting the innocent, his is to find the answer. It sounds dry and heartless, and that's because he is. Well, not heartless, but he just doesn't understand people enough to care about them like you and me."

"You told me he's a good man. How can he be if he doesn't

care about what's right, about helping people?" Julianne's brow wrinkled.

Margit pursed her lips, thinking. Then, she touched a hand to Julianne's head and muttered a word as her eyes turned white. Julianne's vision blurred. When it cleared, she didn't see the room she'd been standing in a moment ago.

She saw a man, older than her, but not ancient. He walked through the Temple halls, past a tapestry she recognized. Instead of faded and moth-eaten, it was bright and clean. The man strode around a corner, not looking up from the book he was buried in.

A young Margit approached him. "Get your head out of that, Art. You'll miss dinner, and I know you didn't have lunch."

"But Megs, I think I've found it! I know why Queen Bethany Anne left, and I think that's why everything changed when she did!"

"Eating first won't make her come back, and sure as hell won't make it so she never left. Come on."

Margit tugged on Artemis's arm, but he resisted. "Don't you understand? I've been looking for this information for years! I can't, I can't stop. Not now. Just… not now." His face was pained and as he spoke, his breathing picked up. Through Margit's memory, Julianne could feel his panic, his worry that stopping now might make him lose it all.

"Ok, Artie. It's ok. You sit here and read, find your answers."

Artemis nodded blankly, his emotions receding as he backed off into a quiet corner, slid down against the wall and sank back into his book. He didn't react to Margit's instructions to stay but, when the vision blipped forwards a little, he did rouse enough to absentmindedly nibble on the fruit and bread she had brought from the dining hall.

"We took care of him as best we could, but we couldn't make him stay." Sadness touched Margit's voice and feelings. "Oh, he could function alright as long as he remembered to eat and bathe, it's just he wasn't very personable. I knew he'd be happier away from here, in a place that's quiet and lonely, but it's hard to really understand that. Even with powers like ours."

Julianne shook her head, wondering how in the world she would be able to get this man to help her. Then, setting her shoulders, she decided it didn't matter. She had to, for the good of her people, so she would. She would find a way.

"That's my girl!" Margit cuffed her under the chin, then pushed herself to her feet. "Now, you get some sleep. You need to meet your escort nice and early, and rearick don't like to be kept waiting."

That was true, Julianne thought with a grimace. She pulled back the bedspread and slipped underneath, determined to relish her last night on a soft mattress. After only a short meditation, she slipped into turbulent dreams.

Julianne stood at the great doors of the Temple. Her people gathered behind her, cheering and celebrating the first steps of her journey and ahead, a horse waited patiently, saddled and ready to take her to the Madlands.

Danil appeared on one side of her, Zoe on the other. "We hope you have a wonderful journey, Master, and return with the help you seek." Zoe kissed the back of her hand and gave a gentle push.

"Master, your horse is waiting." The kind faced rearick smiled and gestured her forwards, but Julianne's heart tore at the thought of leaving her people behind.

"Go on. We'll be fine," Margit said over her shoulder.

Still, Julianne hesitated, poised on the top step, one foot out and a hand on the door frame for balance. She tried to ignore the feeling of wrongness, that this wasn't what she was meant to be doing.

"Where are my bags?" Julianne asked. A tumble of butterflies writhed in her stomach, and she wracked her mind for anything she may have forgotten.

"On the horse," Danil said. "Everything's ready."

Julianne looked into his clear, blue eyes. Her heart reached out to him, but she didn't speak.

"You're nervous," he said, smiling. "Here. I picked these this morning. Your favorite color, for luck." He plucked a pretty purple flower from his pocket and tucked it behind her ear.

Julianne had never seen one like it before, with its deep throat and curled tips. "Where did you find it?" she asked.

Danil laughed. "A pretty little sparrow came to my window this morning. I think it was gathering pretties for a nest, and it left me this. As soon as I saw it, I knew you'd love it."

Ice slammed into Julianne's chest and her eyes widened. This wasn't her dream. Never, in all the years she had known him, had she dreamed of Danil as anything but what he was: blind. Her Danil could not have 'seen' the sparrow, or the flower.

Gasping, she squeezed her eyes tight shut. Forming a wall of stone, she shoved, shattering the small weight that pressed against her mind.

CHAPTER EIGHT

Julianne opened her eyes, and almost screamed. She was perched on her windowsill, one foot out and ready to take a single step that would send her plummeting onto the stones below. She spun, jumping down onto the floor as her attackers still stood, dazed after being shoved so brutally from her mind.

Her movement shocked them awake. Adrenaline pumping, she knew her mind wasn't calm enough for a calculated attack. It didn't have to be. Their defenses were down and even as she pushed an alarm to every mystic in the Temple, she thrust into the mind of the first man.

Normally, mind control was a delicate thing. You didn't want to cause damage, or leave a lasting impression.

Not this time.

Julianne twisted and hammered, severing connections and pulling out virtual wires. The man screamed, his shriek dying down to a gurgled stammer as he fell to the floor convulsing.

His companions looked on in horror until one turned to Julianne. Satisfied her first victim wouldn't be joining the fight again, she went to work on the next, piercing a soft spot in his mind, his mental shield warped by terror.

She fed into it, building paranoia onto the horror of his comrade's death, pulling in the dark of the night and his suspenseful trek through the sleeping Temple. His fear grew, swallowing him.

A noise outside was the final catalyst and he shoved past Julianne, knocking her down as he ran past. Desperate to escape whatever monster he'd helped her create in his mind, he cast himself out the window, his screams ending with a sickening crunch and silence.

Julianne threw her mind at her final attacker, but he'd had time to erect his defenses. He didn't have the impenetrable shield Donna used, but Julianne had burned through a massive amount of energy dealing with his friends.

"Your tricks won't work on me, bitch," he laughed.

"Please…" Julianne took a step backwards, raising her hands.

He moved closer, his greasy smile growing as he watched her plead.

"Please, don't hurt—"

He took one more step and Julianne smirked. She whipped a fist out, punching him square in the nose. Stunned, he reeled back, choking on blood. Her foot was next, snapping up to make contact with his already broken cartilage, then a second one towards the groin.

He doubled over, making it all too easy to plant her knee into his already smashed-in face. Coughing out a splatter of blood, he collapsed onto the floor.

One of the first changes Julianne had made to the teaching curriculum was to add in lessons on how to use magic while also concentrating on other things. She never wanted one of her students to be so confident in their mystic ability that they underestimated a non-magic opponent.

By playing weak and desperate, she had made her attacker buy in to the idea that magic was everything, that without it, she couldn't fight. Then, she hit him—literally—with the last thing he expected.

"Three strikes, *dipshit*," she said, staring over him. This time, the smile was on her face. Her door flung open as she dropped into a fighting stance, quickly relaxing when she saw her own guards piling in.

"Shit on a stick. What the fuck happened in here?" Aldred asked, eyes wide.

"Remember all those lessons I insisted on that had nothing to do with magic?" Julianne asked. Aldred and his companions nodded. "He didn't take them." She pointed at the man on the ground in a heap.

A crowd had gathered down the hallway, but Julianne was too tired to reach out mentally. When a commotion started up behind them and someone shoved through, she flinched, expecting worse news. Relief soaked her bones when she saw Danil. He rushed up to throw his arms around her.

"Are you ok?" he asked. He blinked, white eyes off in the distance. Then, he blanched. "Bitch and Bastard. What the fuck happened to his face? What did he do, call you a girl?"

It was Julianne's pet hate. She wasn't a girl; she was a woman, and Master of the Temple. Anyone who treated her otherwise would get their ass handed to them in short measure.

"I'm fine." Relief drained away as she pushed him back. "But we need to figure out how these men got inside, and if there are any more of them. Where's Gunther?"

"Can't reach him, Master. I sent a runner up to wake him, but he wasn't in his room." Aldred's face creased with worry. "We're missing another, too. Daved couldn't be found when William went to relieve him earlier."

"Why the bloody hell didn't you raise the alarm then?" Julianne snapped. The last guard rotation was at midday.

Aldred shrugged, averting his gaze. "It's not unusual. Daved enjoys the elixir just a bit more than he should. We thought he must be passed out in a hallway somewhere. I'd planned to take him off rotation until he sorted it out. This was his last shift."

Hoping it wasn't his last ever, Julianne mobilized the watching mystics. "Groups of three, scour the Temple first. Stay mind-linked with another group and if anyone drops out, *sound the alarm*. Aldred, you and two others will stay here and look after these two."

Aldred saluted. Before she turned to go, Julianne kicked one of the unconscious men. Not hard, but enough that Aldred winced. "If either of them wake up, let me know."

The crowd in the hallway thinned quickly as mystics—eyes glossing over with white film as they summoned mental links—darted off to search for their missing comrades. The fear in the air was palpable.

Melanie? Julianne sent with some effort. *The children.*

I'm with them now. Would you like us to assist on the search?

As much as a dozen extra eyes would help, Julianne shuddered, thinking of what they may find. *No. Keep them occupied and shielded. Do you want me to send a group to help?*

No, I have two of the guards with me. We'll just practice our emergency drills. Despite Melanie's loathing of violence, it had been her idea some months ago to create emergency practice drills for the children.

They would evacuate to one of the many hidden passages within the Temple and erect the strongest shields they could maintain. Once hidden, they would sink into a silent meditation and reduce their heart rates as low as possible. This would make them all but invisible to anyone searching for them, with or without magic.

Thank you. Julianne sent a flood of gratitude to the woman, who replied with the same. They often butted heads, but each knew the other's sole motivation was to keep their people safe.

An hour later, a loud scream was punctuated by a sensation of overwhelming grief, as the discovery of two bodies was passed through the mystic Temple as fast as thought. Gunther and Daved, throats slit, had been rolled into a bush just outside the gates and covered over with branches.

No. Julianne fought the urge to fall to her knees with grief. *Not Gunther.*

He'd spent more time by her side than anyone since she had taken her position as Master. Heart racing, hoping she was wrong, she sprinted to the gates just in time to see both bodies being laid on the ground.

"*Fuck!*" she screamed as she turned, then punched the stone wall behind her. She leaned into the cold surface, teeth clenched so hard she was sure they'd crack.

Strong hands grasped her shoulders, kneading them. "We'll find them, Jules. All of them. And we'll make sure they pay for what they did." Danil tried to pull her into a hug, but she brushed him off.

Julianne forced her jaw to relax and took a deep breath, hardening her grief into a ball of solid metal. *This,* she thought. *This will drive me harder than any loss I've taken, Donna. You don't know what you've done.*

When Julianne looked up, her eyes were hard. Though tears glittered, they didn't fall. "It doesn't make sense. How did they get to them? They shouldn't have been able to make it past Gunther, no matter how fucked up Daved was on Elixir."

Aldred? Julianne sent to the guardsman. *Either of our friends woken up yet?*

Not yet, they... Julianne felt a spike of alarm from Aldred. *Ahh, shit. Master, I'm sorry, I should've kept a closer eye.*

A quick image flitted through Julianne's mind of Aldred turning over the man she'd fought with. He was grey and lifeless past the smear of blood that saturated his lower face.

A cold weight pressed at her heart. *How?*

Mostly likely suffocated. Aldred's guilt and pain came through the mental link. *I'm sorry.*

Despite the dead man's attempt on her life, Julianne felt a pang of regret for the life wasted. *Not your fault,* she sent. *Bastard came here to kill me. Who knows what else they'd planned?*

Julianne shivered, then nudged Danil. "I have to go back in. Stay here, make sure everyone is accounted for. Could you…" She couldn't form the thought, but Danil understood.

"I'll see to Daved and Gunther. You go. Try not to implode any more heads unless it's needed." Danil leaned in to give her another hug, and this time, she accepted the gesture. It warmed her slightly, and she breathed in his familiar scent, steadying herself.

Danil pulled away and called over another mystic to stand by him and act as his eyes. He directed the guards and others around to hoist the bodies and carry them inside.

CHAPTER NINE

Julianne slipped away quietly, darting to the upstairs room where Aldred waited. He bowed as she entered and tried to stammer another apology.

"I don't need apologies from you, Aldred, I need leadership. You are now Master of the Guard. Take the body, leave the other. You will need to organize your troops and increase the security. At daybreak, come and see me. I will brief you on last night's meeting, you'll need to know about the changes."

Aldred gaped, frozen as he tried to compute the rapid-fire instructions Julianne sent at him. "I'm… Master of the… But Master, I just let a man die under my watch!"

"Bloody hell, Aldred," she replied. "You let a prisoner suffer the fate he was probably intended for anyway. Can't quite put that in the major fuck up column, can we? You're a good man, and I trust you. Right now, I need you. Can you do as I ask, or should I turn the duty over to William? If you accept the position, he will be your second."

Aldred drew himself up and offered a crisp salute. "I will pledge my heart, mind, and soul to you, Master. You can rely on me."

Julianne allowed herself a smile. "For the love, you're not pledging to me, Aldred, but to the mystics of the Heights."

Gunther's oath had simply been 'to the mystics' and Julianne hated that she'd had to make a distinction. The mystics had always been her family; now it seemed that some no longer were.

She shooed Aldred away to his duty and closed her eyes, searching for her center. She found it, not the calm, still pool she normally held, but a lake of frozen ice. She stayed there a moment, honing her mind. Then, her eyes flicked open, white as snow, onto the unconscious man at her feet.

Wake up. She sent the thought with a powerful push, and was gratified when the body twitched. The man rolled, then cracked his eyes open. They drifted over to Julianne's face, then past it, uncomprehending.

Julianne blinked and her eyes cleared. She waited a moment, but he didn't move. She pushed away her familiar headache, muttered a word under her breath, and her eyes glazed over again with white mist.

Then, she dove into his mind.

She coldly examined the damage she'd done. It surprised even her. Julianne was the strongest mystic that lived, according to Selah. It was a hard thing to gauge, but she was clearly leaps and bounds ahead of her more experienced peers. This? This was new.

For a brief moment, she felt regret; Then, Gunther's swollen face came to her own mind. Her angst fading, she pushed through the broken psyche to rifle through the man's memories.

His name was Jared. Even getting that was a trial. As memories floated past, Julianne snatched at them, but most were too torn to make any sense. She saw the back of a farmer's cart, oversized. Probably something from childhood. A meal, something with potatoes, and a snippet of a song caught in a repetitive loop.

A warmth spread over shoulders as he donned a blue robe. Gone. A man, a shadowy figure that came with a sense of pleasure, a gift for doing well. It quickly soured. A crawling like a million ants beneath the skin, light enough that it wasn't pain, but sickening. He had done some-thing wrong, displeased the Master...

Julianne swooped away from his mind, her eyes clearing as she broke the trance. Her legs wobbled, and she sat down on the floor with a thump, then leaned over to press her forehead on the cold stone wall beside her. Despite Margit's warning, she'd overextended herself.

After a moment, the spinning in her head slowed down and she could stand again. Julianne watched him lie on the ground, drool tracing a glistening line across one cheek. Despite his condition, he was more alive than Gunther and Daved, more than she would have been if she'd stepped out the 'door' in her dream.

When she opened the door to her room, the guard outside ducked his head.

"Matthew, ask Aldred what to do with our guest. He won't be a danger, but he'll need babysitting so he doesn't choke on his own tongue. If he lives past morning, I'll decide what to do with him then."

"Yes, Master." The guard's eyes misted over for a minute. "He said the holding cell should be sufficient, there should be someone down there. Are you... well?"

For a moment, she didn't understand the question.

"Sorry, Master. It's just... you look like shit. Worse, even."

An image of Julianne's pale, drawn face and shadowed eyes floated in front of her, projected by the guard.

Screwing up her face, Julianne said, "I'm fine. Just tired. That reminds me, was Aldred on last shift?"

The guard nodded and Julianne cursed herself for slow think-ing. She'd sent the man on a dozen errands when he was already dead on his feet. "Before you take our new resident away, send for William. I need to see him."

Matthew didn't ask why Julianne didn't just send the

messages herself, likely guessing she was mentally exhausted. His eyes whitened again, barely returning to their normal warm brown before boots came jogging down the hall. "He's just—"

"Here," William called as he rounded the corner. "What do you need?"

"No other problems?" Julianne asked.

He shook his head. "Everyone seems to be accounted for. Aldred mind-searched those on duty when the New Dawn crew left. It looked like all five passed through the gate, but Aldred found telltale signs of an illusion. He suggested that was the reason for the robes. Much easier to project a simple hooded figure when you don't have to worry about facial details. We think two left, and these three stayed."

Julianne nodded tiredly. "Tell Aldred he's relieved for the night. I'll wager he needs rest as badly as I do."

CHAPTER TEN

It was another two days before Julianne finally left on her journey. She woke early, still feeling mushy after several late nights spent fortifying the Temple defenses, checking that emergency drills were in place and hoping each night would lead to something other than dreams of falling, dying, or killing.

"You're sure the rearick were ok with rescheduling?" Julianne asked as Margit ran down a checklist of things to be addressed while Julianne was gone.

The older woman would, with the help of the elder mystics and some of Julianne's trusted advisors, take the reins while she was gone. It was only a short-term solution, and Julianne suppressed a shiver of fear, wondering what would happen if she ran into trouble and couldn't return.

"Of course, they were. An extra fifteen percent charged for the privilege of lying about a few more days? The greedy bastards are always ok if it makes their pockets a bit heavier." Margit rolled up the papers and used the hollow tube like a weapon, pointing it at Julianne. "Stop being a ninny. I might be old, but I'm far from dead. I can handle things until you get back, even if you run into delays."

Grinning, Julianne nudged Margit with her shoulder. "Your secret will be out, though. No more playing the frail old lady—they need a strong leader, and you won't be able help yourself."

Margit scowled. "Fine. The cranky old sow persona won't be going anywhere, though. That one's real."

Julianne snorted as she headed for the door, hefting her pack over one shoulder. Months spent in Arcadia pretending to be a guard had given her a new appreciation for physical strength as well as mental, and she'd made sure not to lose it when she'd returned. "If you're going to see me off, we'd best get going. I want to be gone before the sun is fully up."

She took the stairs quickly, barely stopping to give each guard she passed a silent nod or quiet farewell. At the door, Aldred greeted her, his expression pained.

"Aldred, what's wro—oh." By the door, Danil waited for her. She'd expected him to be up in time to say goodbye. She had *not* anticipated him turning up with his bags packed and an extra horse saddled and ready. "Danil, what the hell are you doing?"

Aldred heaved a sigh and fished in his pocket. As he handed over two shiny coins to the blind mystic, he mumbled an apology. "Sorry, Master. Damn fool just showed up and ordered a horse. Threatened to wake the whole Temple if we said no."

"And the bet?" Julianne asked, one eyebrow raised.

"Well, seeing as how close you two are, I figured you'd have guessed at his plans, or read them from him. He said you wouldn't, that you'd been too busy."

"Too trusting, more like," Julianne huffed. "Thank you for your faith in me Aldred, even if it was misplaced this time." The guard nodded, watching sadly as his money disappeared into Danil's pocket.

She turned to Danil, hands on her hips. "This was a solo trip, Danil. We've told the rearick we need a single person escort, not a party of two. I can only imagine the surcharge they'll add on. And anyway, I need you here. You *can't* come.

Your ass is staying in the Heights." She didn't apologize for her order.

"Sorry, Jules." He shrugged, then turned to check that his saddle was fastened correctly. "I'm coming. My feet have been itching to go on a pilgrimage for a while, and I'd planned to go a little after you left anyway."

"But you—"

"Besides," Danil cut her off with an easy smile. "Think how reassured the others will be to know you won't be alone, traipsing across the Madlands." He pressed a hand to his heart. "Think of the children."

"I'll shield you," she threatened. "You won't be able to see where you're going." Julianne knew she wouldn't do that, but damned if she was going to back down without a fight.

"Fine. You know I can make it down the mountain alone, the horses are well trained. Mine will follow yours, until you abandon us. Both of us. A mystic and his loyal horse, frozen to death or maybe drowned, all because they couldn't find their way home." He struck a dramatic pose, one hand to his forehead while the other stretched out beside him.

Julianne let out a howl of frustration. He'd been in moods like this before. She wouldn't be able to convince him to stay, and if she dug her heels in and made good on her threat, he'd try even harder to follow. "You, Danil, are as lovable as the sweaty scrotum of a hairy boar. The boar is better looking, too."

His mouth dropped open, unused to hearing such colorful insults from the Master of the Temple.

"Aldred, will you help me with my pack?" Julianne turned away from him to address the Master Guardsman. While he tied her bags to the horse, Julianne briefly delved into Danil's mind. He was more worried about her than he should be, and not just for her physical safety.

She had, after all, killed two men. Though Julianne had tried hard to block off that part of her mind, to protect the cool confidence she usually wielded when running the Temple, Danil had seen past that.

Her nose prickled and her eyes stung, and she cursed him for making her feel emotions she was trying to ignore.

"All ready, Master. Any last instructions?" Aldred patted the mare's rump, then stood back. He eyed Danil warily, as if wondering if he'd need to restrain his fellow mystic at the Master's request.

When Julianne shook her head, Aldred dropped his eyes for a moment. "It might not be my place to say, Master, but... be careful."

Julianne leaned in for an impulsive hug, leaving the Master Guardsman red as a beetroot. "Take care of our people, Aldred. Margit is strong as a horse and has wisdom even beyond her many years, but she'll need your support."

"Aye, that I will, young man." Margit's tall frame looked willowy in the wide doorway, but she stood tall and strong. Moving over to Julianne, she dropped a peck on her cheek. "I see you've already picked up some road dust," she commented with a sharp glance at Danil. Then, with a wink at Julianne she added, "I assume it's welcome, though."

Despite the chill in the air, heat rose up past Julianne's neck to tinge her cheeks a fiery red. *Shut up, you,* she sent to Margit.

Nothing wrong with a body to keep you warm when you're spending the night on the ground, came Margit's razor-sharp reply.

The thought of rolling around in the dirt with a man brought a very different image to Julianne's mind and she slammed a shield down as fast as she could assemble one. It was too late. Margit's eyes widened like saucers before she broke into a cackling laugh.

And who, exactly, is Marcus?

Julianne didn't dignify Margit's stunned question with a response, instead taking a moment to stifle the thought of the handsome young guardsman she'd become close with in Arcadia.

She cursed internally when a quick glance at Danil showed his face still, shoulders tight as he stared resolutely in another direction.

Oh, hell, Julianne thought to herself. This was going to be one awkward journey.

Aloud, she said, "It's not too late to stay behind, Danil." Julianne tried to keep her tone light. "No warm beds or easy coins where I'm going."

If you're really against me going, I'll leave you be, he sent.

Danil, I... What could she say? She'd known about his feelings for a long time, but it had never affected their friendship. *Please come.*

His face broke into a sunny smile and he kicked his horse, sending it carefully picking its way down the mountain.

"I suppose I better go, before he and the horse end up halfway to Cella. Margit, you'll be ok?" Last minute doubts assuaged Julianne about leaving her tiny community to fend for themselves.

"Be gone with you, girl. We survived alright before you, and we'll do just fine while you're gone."

Julianne waved as her horse made its way after Danil's. Before she was out of sight of the Temple, she found him waiting beside the path.

"Err... thought I'd better let you go first," he called to her.

"Just remember, I can't see behind me," she replied.

"I know. Just remember, I do this every day." He stuck his tongue out at her and Julianne laughed, feeling the tension from earlier drop away.

They took their time, not wanting to rush the horses over the rocky terrain. It took an hour to reach Craigston, by which time both were starving.

"Shall we stop for breakfast first, or meet the rearick?" Danil asked.

"I planned ahead. We're meeting them in Ophelia's." Julianne turned her horse in that direction, after taking a moment to pass her eyes over the small mining town to give Danil a better view of where they were.

Julianne made for a low, stone building, following her nose more than her memory. The smell of sausages wafted out, along with the jumbled sound of several conversations.

Julianne dismounted and tied her horse to a wooden post outside, then helped Danil to secure his. Together, they made their way inside. Julianne wrinkled her nose at the smell of spiced meat and boiled cabbage, then pressed a hand to her stomach as it let out a noisy growl.

Julianne? Danil's soft mental nudge made her jump, enthralled as she was at the smells coming from the kitchen. He directed her attention to a figure in one corner. She quested, then recoiled when she realized the mind was familiar.

"What the hell is he doing here?" she groaned.

CHAPTER ELEVEN

Bastian looked up, alerted by Julianne's brief touch on his mind. He quickly stood, bowing his head to Julianne in a gesture of courtesy. Bastian had butted heads with Julianne more than once.

As a recent graduate, he hadn't yet gone on his own pilgrimage and Julianne had meant to address that before she left. *Oh, I hope this doesn't mean what I think it does,* she thought, careful to keep it behind the mind shield she used almost constantly outside of the Temple.

"Master, I'm glad to see you. I expected you earlier." He shot Danil a brief look of curiosity, but didn't comment.

"And why exactly were you waiting for me here, of all places?" Julianne asked, trying to keep the irritability out of her voice.

"To… well, to join you on your pilgrimage. If that's ok. I mean, the rules do say…"

The rules said a senior mystic must do all they could to facilitate the journey of a new graduate. Julianne was pretty sure that didn't extend to babysitting them along the way. "This really isn't a safe journey, Bastian. We're heading right through the Madlands on a search for a man who may not even be alive anymore. This isn't your typical jaunt through the countryside."

"I've packed for a long trip." His face was eager. "Besides, I plan to break off once we cross the Madlands and take my own journey."

Julianne sighed. She turned her back on Bastian to speak to Danil. "Do you want to wait here while I find the rearick we hired? They're not going to be happy when they find out the party of one they were escorting is now three." Danil nodded, tweaking an eyebrow at Julianne's stark white eyes.

While her face was hidden, she deftly slipped into Bastian's mind. In it swirled the words Donna had spoken about mankind, and their mission to make the world a 'better' place. There was also the hint of resolution, a map of Irth, and the questions he'd asked the barkeep about navigating to the border of the Madlands.

He was unaware of her intrusion, and Julianne took a moment to curse whichever teacher graduated him. Julianne felt her jaw clench. What she'd seen in his head convinced her that even if she forbade him to join her, the stubborn mule of a boy would make the dangerous trek alone.

A cough behind Danil caught her attention. Julianne peered around him to find a rearick, hidden behind the taller mystic, tapping his foot impatiently. "Are you the mystic that hired a guard?" the rearick asked.

"Yes," Julianne said quickly. "But there's been a slight change of plans. There are now three of us."

The rearick scowled. "One of my men can't protect all three of ye. Expect ta be payin' fer more hands, and a fee fer the last-minute change."

Three? You're bringing him with us? Danil slipped the words into Julianne's head.

I don't think it's a good idea to leave Bastian behind just now. I'll explain later.

"That's fine, I can cover the costs. And I'm sorry for the sudden change. It was a… last minute thing."

The rearick lifted an eyebrow, as if wondering how a bunch of mind readers could have so much trouble organizing themselves. Then, he shrugged. "Coins are coins. I'll fetch yer hire and see if I can't find two more. The booking will be tripled, but maybe ye can talk down the hires when ye meet 'em. Group discount, if ye like."

"Tripled?" Julianne asked. "That's ridiculous."

"So is asking fer a one-man hire and needin' three." The rearick stuck his hand out and waggled his fingers.

Julianne dropped the required coins into his palm and he grinned. Though she probably could have talked him down a little, it would have taken time. She was too impatient for that. When the short man wandered off, he was whistling a satisfied tune.

Julianne slid into a seat next to Bastian, Danil taking a seat across from her. An awkward silence fell.

"You lot wantin' food, or nay?" Ophelia yelled. The rearick woman was as burly as her male counterparts.

"Please," said Julianne. "Two plates of whatever's cooking, with some bread, too."

Ophelia looked at her expectantly and Julianne smiled sweetly. "Danil? I'm afraid I only brought enough coins for myself."

The contented smile fell from Danil's face. "You're gonna make me pay for this a thousand times over, aren't you?"

Julianne's smile widened. "If you're lucky, it'll *only* be a thousand."

Groaning, Danil pushed himself up from the table to go and pay for their meal. He laid out his money on the counter, a tactic Julianne had seen him use when he was relying on someone else's eyes to see the coins. After counting a few out and sliding them across the counter, he returned to his seat.

"So, Bastian," he said, stretching his arms out to either side.

"What gave you the bright idea to cross a land of dangerous, ravaging monsters for your first pilgrimage?"

Bastian paled slightly, looking from Danil to Julianne, who just shrugged. Danil's description of the Madlands had been more accurate than she'd like to admit.

"I seek truth," Bastian said, his voice wavering. "I want to know what the world is *really* like, not just what I've been told."

He came from Arcadia, didn't he? Julianne asked Danil.

Not quite. His family had a small estate outside the town, he answered.

Julianne mulled that over. If Bastian's family had been of high station, they would have lived in the middle of the city. Yet, they weren't so poor as to be pushed into the slums. Bastian's family would have dealt with the nobles though, if they'd traded with the city.

"Bastian, I plan to pass Arcadia on my way to the Madlands. Do you have family there you wish to visit?" Julianne wanted to read his thoughts, but she couldn't do that without her eyes changing. The little she'd seen earlier made her want to tread carefully.

"No." His answer was terse and a shadow passed over his face. He buried his nose into his mug.

"Slow down," Danil said with a hint of alarm. "That's not rearick ale, is it?"

That made Bastian chuckle. "Don't think I can handle my liquor? Don't worry. I've heard about the brews down here and I admit, I'd probably be on the floor after one or two. This is just cider."

Danil opened his mouth to reply, but two plates were slapped on their table. Steam wafted from sausages and bacon, with a side of cooling sauerkraut and fresh baked bread. "Enjoy." The cook wiped his hands on a greasy apron and scurried back to the kitchen.

"I believe our hires are here," Danil said.

CHAPTER TWELVE

Julianne swung round to look. Two rearick stood just inside the door. The bearded one lit up in a smile, and Julianne waved to him. "Garrett! You're part of our escort team?" Garrett and some of the other rearick had showed up when the Arcadian rebellion needed them the most. Together, they'd fought off Adrien and made the city a free place again.

"Aye. Not much of a team, though. Old Harker couldn't find anyone but the two of us."

"Well, there might only be two, but we can fight. Worth the price of three, at least." The other rearick was, to Julianne's surprise, female. She looked young, despite the hardened face that came from living in a place like Craigston. The rearick valued hard work and set their children to profitable enterprises at a young age.

"We'll pay for two," Julianne said firmly.

"You've seen me fight, lass. Ye can't be saying I'm not worth at least two on me very own?" Garrett gave Julianne a toothy grin and winked.

"Yes, but I've also seen you eat. The contract said I'm to pay for your services, but also your food. Are you trying to send the

Temple bankrupt?" Julianne schooled her expression, unwilling to let the professional haggler get the best of her.

Garrett slumped. "Fair enough. I suppose I may be worth a man and a half, but Bette here is a woman. That makes her only worth a half. *Ow!*" He flinched and rubbed the shoulder Bette had just punched with a closed fist.

It wasn't a playful jab, either, going by the set of her mouth. "Garrett, you know *bloody* well I can fight just as well as the rest of ye."

"I'm just sayin', women are more suited ta—OW!" A second punch, aimed in the same spot as the first, finally made him close his mouth.

"Two fees, food and lodging for both—of my choosing, mind you—and you're to split it *evenly* between you," Julianne said. "We'll be done eating in a few. Our horses are out the front. Bastian, did you bring one?"

"Yes. Well, I've hired one, but I've yet to pick him up. A fellow named Heston?"

Bette gave a loud snort. "He'll charge ye double for half a nag. Here, I'll ask Bern if his runner is in. No cheaper, but she'll last ye the distance."

"You can go organize that while Danil and I finish up here," Julianne said, dipping her bread into the gravy on her plate. Bastian pushed back his chair, then awkwardly maneuvered past Julianne and headed for the door.

As the rearick turned to follow him, she caught Garrett's arm. She waited until Bette and Bastian had moved away before speaking. "And if I hear one more word about women being 'better suited' for other professions, you'll find yourself returning to the Heights with a penchant for wearing sundresses, you hear me?"

Garrett went white as a sheet. "Yes. Yes, Ma'am." He ran off to join the others.

Danil held in his laughter until the rearick had gone. "Doesn't he realize you can't mind control unless you're standing right by him?"

Julianne sobered. "Danil, that's something that's been bothering me. When I looked into Donna's mind, there was clearly some kind of interference there. Not just the shield. It was like she'd been… controlled. Her thoughts didn't belong to her, not truly, but I don't think it was one of her companions. Is that even possible?"

Danil was silent for a moment, thinking. "How could it be? It must have been one of her people, Jules. Does that mean their leader was there? Was he one of the ones we caught?"

Julianne shook her head. "Danil, I don't think so."

A small handful of rearick entered the room, headed for the bar. They were grimy and flapped their shirts as if to cool down, even though the day outside was bordering on frosty.

"We should catch up with the others," Danil said. "What do you think of Bastian? Clearly, Donna has put some kind of rubbish in his head. Are you sure you want him coming with us into what may turn out to be the heartland of the New Dawn?"

Julianne wrinkled her nose. "When something smells rotten, it probably is. I'd rather him see that now, than let someone beguile him into false ideas that cover the stench in fine perfume."

Laughing, Danil stepped outside, holding the door for Julianne. "You do have a way with words. Very well, we'll take the cub into the lion's den and show him about."

"Keep an eye on him for me? I don't want him to think I'm spying inside his head."

Danil nodded. His need to use magic to see would let him slip in and out of the other man's head without suspicion, though he'd have to tread lightly. Bastian hadn't noticed Julianne's intrusion, but that didn't mean he was completely unskilled.

"Sure, Jules."

As she unhitched the two horses, Julianne reached for her

magic and sent it out to touch the minds around them. She quickly located Bastian and their hired companions. "This way," she said once her eyes had cleared, gesturing for Danil to follow.

Within a few minutes, Craigston was behind them. The town was the end point of the major trade route to Arcadia, so the roads here were wider and better maintained. Garrett led, with Danil beside him. Julianne and Bastian followed, while Bette took the rearguard. Julianne let Bastian ride just a little ahead, slipping into a light trance to see if she could get inside his head again.

He was shielded. Instead of pushing against it, she spoke to him instead. *We're up for a long, hard journey. Are you sure this is what you want?*

I spent my whole childhood on a tiny farm, came the reply. *Then, at the Heights. There's a whole world out there, Master, and all I know of it is what people tell me. I see the mystics who return from pilgrimage and they all see different things. Some like the roads, others hate the dust and rough sleeping. They enjoy the city, with the people and the sights. Others think Arcadia smells, that it's too crowded and dirty. How do I know what's true if I don't see it myself?*

Ah, sent Julianne. *But will your impressions be any more truthful than theirs?* She watched him struggle with that for a moment.

No, but they'll be mine.

Julianne left him to dwell on their conversation for a little while, dropping back to speak to Bette. The young rearick woman had piqued her interest.

"How long have you been working with Garrett?" the mystic asked.

Bette looked down, blushing. "It's my first job. Harker only asked me 'cause he was desperate. He's like most of 'em lugheads back there, thinks a woman's place is in the gardens, or behind a bar."

"What made him change his mind?" Julianne prodded.

"He was desperate! When you lot sprang the change of plans on him, he nearly crapped his damn britches. Couldn't find anyone else, and the only thing worse than sendin' a woman would be givin' a customer back their coins." Then, she frowned. "Why'd you ask me that? I thought you mystics knew everything in a person's head?"

Julianne laughed. "Don't believe everything you hear."

"Well, how's it work then?" Bette asked, curiosity getting the better of her shyness.

"Well... It's hard to explain the *how*, but I can tell you the what. I could read your mind, if I wanted to. Not without going into a trance, though, so my eyes would be white. If you can't see my pupils, that means I'm using my magic."

Bette nodded, considering. "We had a few of yer lot by a few days ago. Their's were almost never clear."

Shock ran through Julianne's nerves like a lightning bolt, along with a feeling of utter stupidity. Of course, the New Dawn would have stopped by Craigston. They'd likely arrived late to the Temple on purpose, knowing it would unsettle the residents. "Tell me about them," she said simply.

"Not much to tell. They came in, looked around. Jones said they bought some of his pretty stones, but not which ones. They weren't friendly, not like you and the rest." Bette paused, thinking. "We figured they must be from somewhere else, with their fancy robes and all."

"Bette, do you mind if I take a peek at what you saw? I just want to confirm something."

Bette paled. "Will it hurt?"

"Not a bit," Julianne said gently. "I promise."

She settled herself on the horse and delved into Bette's mind. Slipping into the thoughts of a non-mystic was only the slightest bit different. Deliberately avoiding anything but what she was seeking, she plucked out Bette's memories of the New Dawn.

Yes, they had been to Craigston. The memories didn't show her anything new, though, just confirmed what Bette had said.

Danil, she sent, *the New Dawn were in Craigston. Can you see if Garrett saw them? Find out what you can.*

Sure, Danil replied. *He just got back from a run to Arcadia, though. Still, he might know something.*

Thank you. Julianne glanced over to see Bette ramrod straight and eyes tightly shut, face pulled into a grimace. "Bette? I'm all done, you know."

"What, already? *Scheisse,* I dinna feel a thing!" A wide grin spread over her face. "What else can ya do?"

For the next hour, she grilled Julianne about the talents of mystics. When Julianne showed her some illusions, and made her feel like her feet were being tickled, she almost fell off her horse with glee.

"Don't I wish I were born special," she sighed.

"Don't be ridiculous," Julianne snapped. "You're the first female Harker sent out on an escort run! You're paving the way for women everywhere, breaking barriers set by those rock-brained men and showing them we can do just as well as they can."

Bette chewed her cheek. "I suppose yer right. I *am* the first woman to work in the guards, and blowed to anyone who thinks I'm worth any less, just 'cause I don't have a dick between me legs!"

Julianne giggled. "Means you'll think more clearly, I bet."

"And I won't be wasting me nights at the taverns, or be taken in by a pretty lass with a thief for a sister like Donovan did, either."

Julianne stretched, regarding her companion with respect. Bette had a damn good point. "You know, if you've got a good head on you, there's a chance you'll have Harker's job one day."

"I dinna want it!" Bette retorted. "It's the road I love. Travelling, seeing new places and earning some coin to do it. I don't mind me a good fight, either."

Julianne didn't remind her this was the first time she had

earned any coin for seeing the world. The girl was pushing against tradition, and Julianne loved that.

It hit close to home, for the Mystic Temple had, like most of Irth, a very male-centric view of the world when Julianne had risen to take Selah's place.

"Things are changing," she whispered, a pool of satisfaction warming inside her breast. When Julianne took the helm back at the Temple, outsiders were often shocked at seeing a woman in control. Then, Hannah had come along and not only proven herself powerful, she'd led an entire revolution.

Julianne opened her mouth to ask Bette what her long-term plans were. Before she could say anything, she was interrupted by voices from ahead.

CHAPTER THIRTEEN

Julianne sent out a mental probe, touching Danil's mind first.

Traders, returning from Arcadia, Danil sent.

Julianne nudged her horse and trotted up to meet them, gesturing Bette to do the same.

"Barton, you're back early," Garrett said, moving his horse to the side of the path.

"Aye. The new designs went better than expected. Seems the people of Arcadia missed our regular trips and are making up fer lost time."

Julianne knew the jewelry trade had suffered during Adrien's rule, the demand for amphoralds overriding the need for pretty things. "I'm glad things are going well for the rearick," she said.

"Oh yes," his companion said with a grin. "The money flows and with all the stones we'd stockpiled, there's more than enough to go 'round. Here," he said, digging in his pocket. "A trinket for ye, lass." He threw something in the air towards Julianne, sending a sprinkle of light over the ground as the sun caught the stone's facets.

The tiny butterfly pin, set with green stones, nestled in Julianne's palm. "How much?" she asked, enamored with it.

"A pretty smile, is all. Them ladies are wanting lizards and fruit this season, not insects, so it won't fetch a price worth more."

Despite an urge to roll her eyes, Julianne grinned. "Thank you," she said, fastening the pin to her robes. "Bette, is it straight?"

"What? That you Bette?" The rearick who'd gifted the stone to Julianne craned his head around to see.

"What of it, Gus?" Bette snapped.

He laughed, a deep, rollicking chuckle. "Aye, that's the spirit. Good to see Sylvan finally broke down. We'd best be moving on, though, want to have tomorrow's load ready to go before nightfall."

Gus nodded to his companion, who had a faraway look in his eyes. Barton absentmindedly kicked his horse, and started past the mystic's party. He paused by Julianne and met her eyes.

His glare bored into her, making the skin on her neck prickle. She debated slipping into a trance, but instead asked, "Anything the matter, friend?"

The rearick frowned and flicked his head. "Just feel like I've forgotten… that pin, where did you get it?" He'd lost his earlier joviality and now sounded flat and toneless.

Confused, Julianne looked down at the green butterfly. "This? Gus just—"

"THIEF!" Barton lunged at Julianne, yanking on his horse's reins violently. The nag shrieked and reared up, her front feet pawing at Julianne.

Julianne fell to the ground and rolled to avoid her own mare's clattering hooves. She pressed up against the rock face as Barton vaulted off his horse. Behind him, Gus screamed "Thief!" over and over, waving his sword in a frenzied pattern.

Barton slammed a fist into Julianne's face. Pain flared from cheekbone to temple. Someone screamed. Julianne threw up an arm to fend off the next blow and caught the brunt of it on her forearm. In that moment, she slipped into a trance.

She shoved against the block on Barton's mind. Her energy was scattered, not strong enough. Pain shot through her shoulder as another blow landed. Bette screamed, two desperate words. "Please, no!"

Drawing her fear, her anger, her pain into a tight ball, Julianne found her center. She pushed the focused energy through Barton's mind, shattering the defenses that kept her out before. She wasn't alone.

"GET OUT!" she shrieked, using all her strength to eject the foreign presence that altered his thoughts.

Barton fell. Julianne was yanked back into her body as he lost consciousness. Reeling, she looked up to see Gus lying in the dirt, in a dark, sticky pool. Bette leaned over him, hands pressed to his shoulder as he moaned.

Garrett yelled. "Ye silly girl, get off him before he kills ye!" His sword was drawn and streaked with blood.

"Don't be stupid, Garrett," she snapped back. "It's alright, Gus. Just breathe, it's not that bad."

Gus turned his head, his eyes darting around in panic.

Eyes clouded over again, Julianne searched. *Where are they?* Julianne pushed the thought to Danil and Bastian. Both men stood ready for battle, eyes white.

I can't find them, Jules. The fear in Danil's voice shook Julianne to the core.

"Garrett, Bette, search the area," she snapped, pulling herself to her feet.

The two rearick eyed each other, then shook their heads. "I canna leave Gus," Bette said.

"I'm not leaving until he's tied up," Garrett said.

Julianne pulled herself up and went to examine the fallen trader. "What happened?"

Julianne gently pushed Bette aside and replaced the rearicks hands with her own. The blood was slowing now.

Garrett's jaw clenched. "He went crazy, attacked Bette. She dropped her sword, couldn't defend herself. I had no choice."

Bette snarled and snatched her weapon from the ground, her hands still slick with blood. She stormed up to Garrett and shoved him, hard. "You *idiot*. I didn't drop me sword, I threw it away so I wouldn't hurt him!"

Garrett shook his head, confused. "He was gonna to kill ye!"

"No he bloody wasn't, he was gonna get a sore bloody head. What the hell were ye thinking, busting in like that? Ye should have been lookin' after *her*!" Bette thrust the sword in Julianne's direction for emphasis.

"Bette, don't be stupid. Gus went crazy! You were unarmed; what the bloody hell did ye want me to do?"

"Use yer thick head, that's what, and stop treating me like I'm a piece of bloody glass. Ye know I can hold me own in a bare hand fight. Gus didn't draw; he just flew at me. It was obviously some kind of mental heebie jeebie, I didn't want to kill the poor bastard."

"Mental… what? Is that what happened?" Garrett swung round, looking to Julianne for confirmation.

Before she could answer, Bette snapped, "Of course, it bloody was. What, did ye think he just didn't like me hat?"

Garrett stared at her for a moment. "Ah, hell. Now I've gone and done it. Gus? Ye with us now, ye bastard?"

"Urmph." The grunt was all Gus seemed to be able to manage. He'd watched the exchange between Bette and Garrett with rising fear, his heart beating faster as blood leaked out of his wound. He tried to sit, but Julianne pushed him back down.

Julianne muttered a quiet word and her eyes turned white. Gus relaxed, slumping back on the ground. "There you go. No need to fret, we'll sort it all out."

"I… I dinna mean to…" His eyelids fluttered.

"Aye, son. We know." Bette patted his good shoulder.

CHAPTER FOURTEEN

Bastian watched Bette take over the first aid duties, binding Gus's shoulder with a bandage from her pack. Danil led Garrett away, quietly explaining what had happened. No one went out of sight, and the mystics kept shooting quick glances at their surroundings, looking out for more trouble.

Dropping into a light trance to keep watch for anyone approaching, Bastian wandered over to Julianne. She'd moved to sit by the sleeping Barton. A dark bruise was forming on her face, and she reached up, wincing as her fingers probed it.

As soon as she had been attacked, Bastian had touched her mind, a technique drummed into students at the Temple. At any sign of crisis, make contact with anyone you can, they said. He'd seen her reaction, the way she'd taken all the things that should have ruined her focus and instead turned them into fuel for her concentration.

He'd watched in awe as she shattered whatever trick had been used to cloud Barton's mind, and the precision she'd used to avoid damaging his true self. It was never a sure thing, but Bastian would lay money on Barton waking up in minutes, alive and well. As if to prove his point, the rearick twitched, then mumbled something.

"Will he be alright?" Bette called from Gus's side.

"I think so. He'll have a headache for a few days like he went on a three-day bender, and his memory of today might be a bit spotty. He'll get off lighter than me," she said wryly. Julianne took Bette's hand and looked in her eyes. "Someone got into their heads, made them think we were roving thieves. Bette, this is important: your friends thought we were someone else. They didn't know who we were, or remember we'd just spoken."

"I still don't know what in the hell happened. Ye saying one of yer mystic people bamboozled me head?" Gus asked.

Julianne nodded. "You attacked Bette. Barton tried to kill me. I knocked him out mentally, but he'll be ok."

"Aye," Bette said. "I'm sorry for knockin' ye about, Gus. And I know Garrett's sorry for stabbin' ye in the shoulder. Silly bastard thought he was helpin'."

"I dinna mean it. Really. For a minute, I was sure ye were bandits, but that makes no sense, does it?" Gus whipped his head around as Bette tried to hold him still.

Bastian, still riding inside Julianne's head, felt the tendril of soothing calm she sent his way.

It must have cost her. Sending emotion like that wasn't an easy thing to do, and Julianne had just expended a huge amount of energy to free Barton from the illusions forced into his head. A distance in Julianne's eyes betrayed her strain and Bastian realized with a shock that her shields were entirely down.

I've got little left, she admitted, finally noticing him in her head. *Do you mind sticking around? I don't think I could fight off a direct attack right now.*

Bastian's heart skipped a beat.

The Master of all his people had just invited him into her unshielded mind, asked him to protect it. It was an honor and responsibility he'd never expected to have, and certainly one he didn't feel confident he could live up to if something did happen.

And yet, her confidence in him was absolute. He could see that. Her thoughts fed off his, and he was unable to ignore the tired musings that flashed through her mind. She'd seen his curiosity about the New Dawn and guessed at his plans to seek them out.

Embarrassed, he tried to turn his mind away from the subject, but Julianne was still on it. She felt in her heart that she was right to be wary of them, but wanted to give Bastian the chance to make up his own mind. And, yes, she wanted to keep him close enough that she'd be there if he got into any trouble.

That confused him. As a student, going through the initiate and intermediary stages of his training, he'd had very little to do with Julianne in a personal sense. She was just too busy, and then had disappeared to Arcadia for months. Why would she care?

Her thoughts caught his and immediately, she answered. *I care about all of you, Bastian.*

The quick flood of memories bypassed him too quick to make out details, but he knew that Julianne thought of every single one of the mystic students as her own, to protect, teach and provide for as a mother would for her children.

He tore his eyes away, distancing himself just enough to pull out of her memories and thoughts while still keeping a watchful eye on her safety. His determination to seek out this strange clan of mystics was beginning to feel foolhardy and disloyal. He wasn't quite ready to give it up yet, though.

He'd tried to learn as much as he could about the events in Arcadia. Nothing he'd heard answered his real questions, though. If the people in power could be so easily corrupted, what hope did the world have? For a fleeting moment, Donna had seemed to present an answer.

Danil and Garrett returned. Garrett led a horse over to Gus. Scuffing his feet in the dirt, he apologized over Gus's protestations that he really didn't need to. As the two rearick started an argument over who was sorrier, Danil wandered over to Julianne and Bastian.

Danil sat with a thump next to Julianne. "You look like you've been hit by a rampaging donkey," he said.

"Always the compliments," she replied. Her mouth quirked up in a one-sided smile.

"We need to get that seen to," he said, tentatively touching the bruise on her face.

"No, we don't. I'm not stubborn enough to risk my health, Danil, but there's no concussion and the bones are all intact."

"Oh, we've picked up a whole new kind of magic, have we? Seeing your own bones?" One eyebrow lifted, the effect made comical by his misdirected gaze.

"Shut up, you. I promise, if it needs to be seen when we get to Arcadia, I'll do something about it then."

"It may not be that simple." Danil's voice dropped a little as he glanced over at the two rearick. "What are we going to do about these two?" He nodded at Gus. "Could turn into a shitstorm if they blame us."

"Why would they?" Bastian asked, startled. "Gus knows what happened. Why would he lie about it?"

Julianne's face was serious. "Bastian, mystics have always been one group. We're split up and we wander around, but we've never had anyone splinter off like this. When two wounded rearick go back to Craigston and tell them mystics were at fault… well, it could get difficult, that's all."

Bastian chewed his lip. "That doesn't seem fair," he said.

"Danil, can you give Barton a nudge? He's almost awake."

Danil's eyes clouded for a moment. Then, mumbling loudly, Barton woke. He rolled to his hands and knees, then sat back. Muzzily looking at the somber faces around him, Barton rubbed a hand over his face, then spat.

"All right, what 'appened? Last I recall, I was on me horse and you had a pretty face." He gestured to the now vicious bruise on Julianne's cheek.

Silence greeted his question. Then, Garrett came to stand over Barton. "Ye almost killed Julianne."

"Bullshit," Barton staggered to his feet, but stumbled sideways, almost tripping over. He caught sight of Gus, who'd fallen into a light sleep. At the sight of the blood, he reeled. "Gus? What' wrong wi' Gus?"

"Barton, he's fine. Please, sit down so we can explain." Julianne's words had no magic behind them, but her status as the Master still had weight. Barton plonked himself back down, eyes darting to the limp form of his friend.

"Ye sure he's not dead?"

"Shh," Bette hissed. "Would you lot keep it down? I just got him to stop *bloody* wriggling." Then, she realized who she was talking to. "Oh, err… good to see you alive, Barton. But shut the hell up!"

"We were attacked by a band of rogue mystics," Julianne explained after Barton was satisfied Gus was safe. "They fooled you into thinking we were brigands, so you tried to fight us. There was… an accident."

"Brigands. Aye, I recall. They took me gold and all our gems. It was after we passed ye… But… we never did, did we?" Barton shook his head as if trying to dislodge an insect from his hair. "Gus?"

"He tried to kill Bette. I stabbed him with me sword. Got his shoulder pretty bad." Garrett stared at the ground, unwilling to meet his kinsman's eyes.

"Fuck it to hell," Barton said, then looked at Julianne. "Sorry, lass."

She shrugged. "You're right. Fuck it all the damn way to hell. This is a shitty situation."

Barton 's eyes widened, then he let out a loud laugh. Bette

chucked a pebble at him, barely missing his head. "You mystics aren't half as stuffy as ye pretend to be, are ye?"

"You should see her when she's in a bad mood," Danil said. "The things she comes out with would make a dead sailor turn in his grave."

Barton snorted, then dropped back into seriousness. "The bloody powers that be up at Craigston will have a blue fit. They've lost a lot of their reliance on the mystics—no offense, love—and I don't know how they'll take this."

"That depends on what they hear," Julianne said quietly.

Barton shot his head up, then leaned closer for a look at the purple swelling below her eye. "Ah, the Bitch take my ever-living soul. There's a mark right in the middle of that mess, a little star. That's me ring." He flexed his fingers, showing off the trinket he wore on one finger.

Julianne probed the indentation. She could feel the little jagged dent in her face. "Don't blame yourself, friend."

"Can't say I remember any of it, but seems you're tellin' the truth, lass. Far as I can tell, we surely were set upon by a group of miscreants, and yerself and yer friends here offered aid where ye could. That's the tale I'll be tellin' on my return and blowed if anyone doubts it, for it's the truth."

"Thank you, Barton." Julianne's shoulders dropped and some of the tension went out of her face. "Do you think Gus will be willing to back that up?"

"Aye, if ye stop yer jabbering long enough for me head to stop thumping," Gus grumbled. Bette lifted her arms in exasperation as he tried to sit up again. This time she didn't bother trying to stop him.

"It's settled, then," Barton said. "We want no quarrel with ye, lass. Be appreciated if you catch the fuckers that caused this shit-storm, though."

"We will," Julianne said. Her eyes glittered with anger. "And we will make them pay."

Bastian wondered how things had become so twisted. Why should the rearick have to lie on their behalf? They were mystics, they should be trusted above all. They'd done nothing wrong, and if word got out that they'd tried to cover this up, it would be a heavy blow to their reputation as a people.

Easy, Danil sent and Bastian pulled his thoughts in immediately.

Aloud, Danil asked, "Is there anything we can do to help you on your way? We'd offer to come back, but under the circumstances, it might be safer if you weren't around us for now."

"Garrett can help me onto me horse," Gus said. "Seeing as he near took me arm off and all. Oh, pipe down, lad. If what yer saying is true, I owe ye for not taking me head when it came down to it."

"You lot be on your way," Barton said. "Won't take us long to get back. If Gus starts leaking again, I'll just send one of the horses back alone. That'll bring a rescue crew down looking."

"I can't thank you enough for offering to keep this quiet," Julianne said. "Whoever caused this tragedy was after us. After me, most likely. You were just caught in the crossfire." She reached a hand out and placed it on the Barton's knee. "Please, accept our deepest apologies."

Garrett helped Gus on his horse, then slapped the nags rump to send her on her way. The group stood watching the two-horse procession leave until they'd rounded a bend and slipped out of sight.

"We shouldn't have to run like criminals," Bastian blurted out when they'd gone.

Garrett shot him a filthy look and pulled himself up onto his horse. "Easy to say when the blood's not on yer own hands, mystic." He kicked his heels and trotted off to wait further down the road.

Bastian looked to Julianne for support.

"The world isn't that simple, Bastian." She, too, mounted her horse. "We could stay and explain, but that could take days. There might be some who doubt our story, and that could start ill feeling to fester between our people. Others will want to ride out and seek revenge, which could put our own mission at risk."

"Our mission?" Bastian asked.

Whatever Julianne had planned, she'd managed to keep it from her thoughts well enough to hide it from him. He stuck his foot in a stirrup and pulled himself up, moving his horse off at a gentle walk beside Julianne.

"I planned this pilgrimage long before the New Dawn showed up. However, the man I'm in search of may have more than just the key to unlocking more of my own magic. He was last seen across the Madlands, where the New Dawn group we saw came from. I need to get out there, Bastian. I need to see what these people are doing, and how their leader got such a tight hold over Donna's mind, seemingly from so far away."

"What?" Bastian started. "Donna wasn't mind controlled. I mean, she had a strong shield, but she acted too normal and calm to have someone in her head."

"What I saw in the brief moments I penetrated her shield was anything but calm, and it *definitely* wasn't normal. I don't understand it, but even so, I can see its danger." Julianne sighed. "Look, I know you think their argument is good. She was persuasive, I get that. What she left out is that there is good and bad in all people. When you have a skill like ours, it's easy to think we know best, that we can run people's lives better than they can themselves."

"So, why are you so against them?" Bastian asked, a sullen set to his mouth.

"Because they're *wrong*, Bastian. Even when we glimpse the deepest thoughts of a person, we don't see the full picture. We can't. And even if we could, even *if* we could create a utopia where people didn't fight and everyone was safe, it wouldn't be right. Do you understand?"

Bastian shook his head. "What can be more important than safety?"

"Freedom. The freedom to make choices, even bad ones, the freedom to make mistakes."

Bastian made a frustrated noise and kicked his horse into a trot, moving up to ride beside Garrett. Danil dropped back to make room for him.

"Don't be bringing yer mood up here, lad. I've enough salt fer the five of us," Garrett muttered.

"Answer me something, rearick. What's more important, freedom or safety?"

"Askin' me won't help ye make up yer own mind." Garrett spat, avoiding eye contact with Bastian.

"Then how am I supposed to?" the young mystic grumbled. "I've spent my whole life locked up in a Temple."

"Tell me, boy, why'd the Master's party suddenly jump from one to three? What happened that made her need two extra bodies with her?"

"You think she *needed* me?" Bastian snorted. "I snuck out to see if I could join her. I knew they'd say no if I asked first, and I was sure I'd be sent back when she saw me."

"So, you could say… you traded safety for freedom? Seems to me you've already made up yer mind."

Bastian gaped, realizing he'd walked straight into that trap. He should have read the rearick's mind before falling for it. Bastian dove into Garrett's mind, only to find there had been no trap, no tricks. Garrett had simply spoken his mind.

Bastian rode in silence, thinking over what he'd said.

CHAPTER FIFTEEN

The delay meant a hard ride to get to the first waypoint before dusk. Designed for rearick travelers hauling goods to the city, the waypoints were set up assuming visitors left in the early morning. Luckily, Julianne's party weren't lugging wagons.

They reached the campsite tired and, at least for the mystics, sore. None of the three had ridden recently, though Julianne was in better shape than the others. She helped Garrett and Bette set up the campsite as Danil prepared a fire.

"Need a hand?" Bastian crouched down next to Danil, offering the other man his sight.

"Better yet, why don't you do it?" Danil suggested.

Bastian leaned over as Danil instructed him. He set up the kindling and wood, then struck the flint to spark the fire. He got it first try. The fire blossomed, chasing away the lengthening shadows and banishing the evening chill.

"Watch out," Danil whispered loudly. "If Julianne sees how good you are at that, she'll drag you along every trip."

Bastian laughed nervously. "I doubt that. I'm pretty useless out here. It's nothing like being in the Temple." He shivered as a cool breeze made the fire flicker.

"You'll adjust." Garrett walked over to drop a heavy pack beside Bastian. "There's yer bedroll. You reckon ye can handle unrolling it? The piss tree is that one, but I'm not helpin' ye with that."

Danil chuckled as Bastian turned red. "I'll be fine, rearick." Bastian picked up his pack and took it to the nearest of the two tents. The soft fabric did nothing to disguise the hard rocks and sharp sticks on the ground below and Bastian groaned, not relishing the thought of laying on it with only a thin mattress to protect his hide.

"Here, set ours up, too, will ye?" Garrett lobbed two more packs in and Bastian obediently rolled them out, squishing them in side by side. When he was done, he returned to the fire.

"...and after I saved her hide, she had the nerve to tell me it was my bloody fault." Garrett stared into the fire, oblivious to Bastian's return.

"Perhaps she really did know what she was doing." Danil's soft voice reached out over the crackling sticks.

Bastian slipped into Garrett's head to get a handle on the conversation. The rearick was tearing himself apart, not just having injured his friend, but his conflicted feelings towards Bette.

Rearick culture was very traditional when it came to gender roles. Garrett's tentative attraction to his colleague gave him an urge to protect her, keep her away from danger and the sort of hardships the men faced.

Though rearick women were no strangers to hard work, and deeply respected for their management skills, they were rarely seen in male-dominated jobs like the guards.

And yet, he'd seen her fight. He knew she excelled in hand-to-hand combat and could probably beat even him. That caused a discomfort and Garrett couldn't get to the root of it. Bastian could. His detached view of Garrett's emotions made it easy to spot. Garrett admired her, even thought she'd be an excellent leader

However, he also wanted to protect her, keep her safe. His worry was distracting him to the point it was dangerous, and his twisted logic couldn't reconcile the two versions of her.

Frustrated at his inability to fix Garrett's problem, Bastian threw a small branch on the fire. "How long until we reach Arcadia?" he asked, hoping to get Garrett's mind off Bette.

"Late afternoon, if we travel well." Bastian's ploy worked, as Garrett's mind immediately ticked over to planning the next day. They would leave early, pack quickly and travel through until lunch time, stopping to eat and rest the horses a short while before moving on.

"Bastian, how long since you passed this way?" Danil asked.

"Years. I was only nine when I was brought here. I only remember it raining. And raining, and raining…" Three days of rain, in fact, and a wet, muddy climb up the mountain.

"Lucky it wasn't snow," Garrett said. "One year, a cold snap hit right at the end of the season and froze the melting sludge. It got real slippery, and we lost two men that went right over the damn side. 'Course, one was drunk and the other was tryin' to sled down the Heights. He might've been drunk, too, come to think of it."

"I knew rearick ale was bad, but didn't realize it'd drive a man to suicide," Danil chuckled.

Garrett eyed him. "Our ale is the best in Irth. 'Course, it takes a real man to appreciate it proper. Or even a good woman, if she's got any taste. Not like the lolly water yer friends drink up the hill. Ours will put hair on yer chest!" He thumped his chest for emphasis.

"Would you lot stick a sock in it?" Bette's yell from the second tent made all three men jump, then burst into hysterical laughter. "I mean it! We're tryin' to bloody sleep in here!"

With incredible effort, the laughter ceased, only to start all over again when Garrett mouthed 'stick a sock in it' with pursed lips and one hand out like a posh lady.

"If you three don't shut up, I'll send you to sleep where you're sitting." Julianne's threat had a little more weight to it and suddenly, Danil yawned.

"Oh, shite, did *she* do that?" Garrett whispered.

"No, but she bloody will in a minute if you don't can it." The side of the women's tent bounced as something was thrown against it inside.

With much snorting and chuckling, the fire was banked and vacated. As Bastian tucked himself in, he heard murmuring beside him.

"The only way you two will be able to work together is if she has your respect, friend. If she thinks you don't trust her as much as you would any of the men, she'll come to hate you."

"Aye. It'd be easier if she weren't so damned pretty."

Bastian rolled over and slept, only to dream of gargantuan women crushing the houses and streets of Arcadia, all because the men around them didn't think that they could.

CHAPTER SIXTEEN

They reached the gates of Arcadia just as Garrett predicted. The steady ride and short break went without interruption and when they arrived, tired and sweaty, they were waved through the gates without hesitation.

"Please," Julianne caught the sleeve of a guard. "I must speak with the Chancellor. Could you let her know that Julianne, Master of the mystics seeks an audience? I'm staying at the Queen's." She ducked her head to hide her eyes, then gave the instruction a mental shove, lodging it into his head.

The guard blinked, then nodded. "My shift ends in an hour, ma'am. I'll be sure to deliver your message directly."

"Thank you, Earle."

Earle opened his mouth, intending to ask how she'd known his name, but she was already gone.

The Queen's Inn was crowded, but the press of bodies parted for the small party as they entered.

"I see the general feeling towards mystics hasn't changed since I was last here," Danil muttered. He hadn't been to Arcadia since Adrien had been in power.

"You didn't see how bad it got," Julianne said. She spoke aloud, uncomfortable displaying her power in the crowded room. Danil didn't have a choice, he needed his magic to navigate the city. If she joined him, though, and if Bastian's eyes went white as well, she worried the situation would go from uncomfortable to downright hostile.

"Should we find somewhere else?" Bette asked.

Julianne shook her head. "We'll get the same reception wherever we go. Mystics are tolerated in Arcadia now, but we'd best not press our luck."

"Well, then, best we'd see if they have room for all of us." Bette looked questioningly at Garrett and he nodded for her to go. She headed for the bar as the others found a vacant table.

A few moments later, she returned with a jug of water and a tray of glasses. "Looks like we got here just in time," she said, taking a seat. "There are two rooms left. You boys will have to share and one of you lucky bastards gets a mattress on the floor."

All eyes went to Bastian, who groaned. "Right, I'm the youngest. I get it."

Danil chucked him on the shoulder. "Atta boy. You're learning."

A young girl darted up to the table. "Sorry for the wait, ladies, gentlemen. Can I get you some wine, or something to eat? We have a fine cheese platter, or some cold meats if you're in need of a light meal."

Julianne regarded the pink cheeked beauty. "You're a little young to be working a bar room, aren't you?"

The girl ducked her head. "I'm finished with my schooling for the day and Aunt Grace says it's the best way to learn the workings, my lady. I'm to have the inn when I come of age. It was my Da's, but he…" her eyes darted away and Julianne's heart tore. The people of this city had lost so much in recent times.

"I'll take some wine, please, and the cheese sounds lovely." A quick chorus of voices joined in requesting wine and mead from around the table. Julianne handed the girl some coins.

"She shouldn't be working in a place like this," Bastian muttered as she ran off to fill their order.

"And what *should* she be doin', then? Wasting her time on pretty dresses and boys?" Bette shook her head. "That girl is making her future, and she'll do well with it if she keeps it up."

"Bette, it's a *bar*. She's not even old enough to drink!" Bastian clamped his mouth shut as the girl in question returned, expertly twisting through patrons with a wide tray.

She set it down and placed the mead and four glasses on the table. "If I'm not mistaken, sir, you ain't old enough to drink either." She gave a pointed look at the empty spot in front of Bastian, who hadn't ordered a drink. "I suppose it's lucky I'm serving the wine instead of drinking it, hey?"

Bette gave a whoop of laughter as the girl strode off, head high. "And what did I tell ye? Lass has every right to be workin' in the business her Da left her, and you've no right to be complaining about it. Would ye have said anything if she were a boy instead?"

The answer was evident by the scarlet blush that crept up his face. "That's different," he said without conviction.

"And what do you think, Garrett?" Bette asked, a dangerous glint in her eye.

Garrett missed the glint, and the sensible warning that his brain screamed came just a moment too late. "Bastian is right; this is no place for a wee lass like that."

"And a wee lad?" Bette leaned forward on the table, glaring.

"Well... I mean... no? Kid should be learning or playing games, lad or lass." Garrett winced, then heaved a sigh of relief as Bette relaxed back into her seat.

The company ate and talked, mostly about the city and the changes it had seen recently. Since Adrien's downfall, the new Chancellor had been scrambling to bring Arcadia back into some kind of order, while undoing the damage its old leader had wrought over the common people. The reports Julianne had received were promising, though.

Danil stood, almost tipping the table over in his haste. He waved an arm and called out, "Over here!"

A young man, sweat beading on his forehead, caught Danil's wave and trotted over. "Message from the chancellor's office. I'm looking for Julianne?"

Julianne nodded and reached out to take the message. "Thank you for bringing it so quickly."

"Ah, no need for that. It's my job." He sketched a quick bow and took off again, doubtless on another errand.

Julianne cracked the fat red seal on the envelope. "I'm to meet with her right away," she said in surprise.

"You'll need to wash up, first," Bastian blurted. Cursing his fat mouth, he added, "No disrespect, Master, but you've been on the road all day."

"That I have." Julianne stood, gulping down the last of her wine with a grimace. "They certainly don't make it like they do back home," she murmured before setting down the cup and going to clean up.

When she emerged from her room, Garrett was waiting. He'd combed his hair and put on a clean shirt. "Yer not going through the streets of bloody Arcadia by yerself, not on my watch. Besides, I haven't seen Amelia in a good while."

Sensing his resolve even without magic, Julianne just nodded. "Of course, Garrett. Thank you."

Look after those two, Julianne sent to Danil as they passed back through the common room.

Bastian's exhausted, Danil sent back. *I'd wager he won't make it more than fifteen minutes before heading to bed. Say... two gold coins?*

You're incorrigible. He was right though, Bastian had slipped into the glassy eyed stare of someone who was only minutes away from much needed sleep.

CHAPTER SEVENTEEN

Julianne stepped out into the cold evening air and shivered. "Yes," she said, reading Garrett's mind. "I should have brought my cloak."

Garrett laughed. "Aye. I wasn't going to say it out loud, so ye canna blame me for thinkin' it."

"It's sensible advice," Julianne admitted. They walked quickly, footsteps echoing through the quiet night. "It's late for a meeting. I wonder why she didn't want to wait until morning?"

"Perhaps Arcadia has had trouble of the sort we saw in the Heights," Garrett suggested.

Julianne didn't answer, and they walked in silence. The streets were empty except for the odd patrol of soldiers, and some staggering drunks. A cat screeched, making Julianne jump before it ran off into the night and a loud argument a few streets over carried through the night air.

"And people wonder why we hate the bloody city," Garrett sighed.

"It's certainly different from home," Julianne remarked.

They walked on, only to stop when a stifled cry caught their attention. They paused.

"Over there," Garrett said in a low voice. He gestured to a dark alleyway. "Wait here."

"To hell with that," Julianne said. She didn't bother to lower her voice as she darted over to the entrance.

The moon was bright enough to illuminate the narrow street, where a tall man stood against the wall. "Stay still, bitch, or it'll hurt all the more when I fuck you."

"Step back, pig fucker," Julianne called.

The man spun, letting the woman he'd had pressed against the wall fall to the ground. She heaved a sob, then scrambled to her feet. Her footsteps slapped on the cobbled road as she fled.

"Oh, you want a turn, too? I'll fuck you so hard your teeth'll hurt." He grabbed his nuts, which dangled freely from his unlaced pants.

"Love your cock, don't you?" Julianne asked, smiling.

"You'll love it, too, if you give it a chance." The man grinned. "Tell ya friend to piss off before I knock his head off. Then I'll show ya why I love my cock so much, bitch."

Garrett hefted his sword, but Julianne waved him down.

"Must be a mighty fine cock," she said as the man shuffled closer, hand still grabbing his bulge. "Why don't you give it a squeeze?"

The man stopped, his hand tightening. His eyes widened as his arm started jerking. "What… what the fuck?" He bent over, wrestling with himself.

"Squeeze tighter," Julianne said, her voice hard as stone. "Squeeze it until it pops."

"What? I… *ahhh*!" He whimpered in pain and crumpled to the ground.

"Come on. We don't want to watch this." Julianne turned and took Garrett's arm, the rearick's face white in the moonlight.

The whimpers behind them turned to screams of pain for a minute, then cut off.

"You… you let him go?" Garrett asked.

"Oh, hell no," Julianne said. "He probably passed out from the pain. He won't be sticking that dick in anyone ever again."

They walked on, Garrett swallowing dryly.

When they reached the offices, an aide named Marie greeted them. "The Chancellor apologizes for pulling you out so late, but it was the best time."

"I understand," Julianne reassured her, thinking back to the days after Selah had passed away. They'd slipped by so quickly, buried under a sea of work.

"Julianne!" Amelia flung open a door and stepped out, ushering Julianne inside. The women shared a brief hug. Garrett refused the invitation into the Chancellor's office, instead taking a seat in the hallway outside.

"I'm so sorry for the short notice, Amelia." "Oh, it's fine." Amelia said as she waved a hand in the air. "You have *no* idea how happy I am to see you. So much has happened and even more has changed. We've rebuilt the factory and had to set up a whole new trade industry to fund the restoration of the city."

"The work seems to agree with you." Julianne was pleased to see the healthy flush on her friend's cheeks, and the sparkle of excitement in her eyes, though something seemed a bit off— maybe even forced.

Amelia grinned. "It's a lot of work, but it was worth it. Seeing it all come together like it did and knowing how we impacted the people in the city was incredible.."

There was a pause before Julianne said, "I couldn't help but notice that you used a lot of past tense there. *Was* incredible?"

Looking down to her desk for a moment, Amelia said, "There is so much happening. I want to tell you, but I also just wish we could have a normal visit."

Julianne forced a smile, and hated herself adding more to Amelia's plate. "It sounds like we have a lot to discuss. I'm just passing through, Amelia, but I needed to speak with you. I have things that need my immediate attention as well."

A look of concern crossed Amelia's face. "You first. You went out of your way to come here. It must be important."

Without hesitation, Julianne said, "There was… an incident up at the Temple."

Amelia sat, and gestured for Julianne to do the same. "That must have been one hell of an *incident* for you to have come here in person."

Julianne nodded. "A group calling themselves the New Dawn appeared a few days ago. I don't know who's leading them, but they're crazed, convinced that mystics are the only ones fit to rule. They want that rule to be absolute."

"Shit." Amelia shook her head, thinking of Adrien's rule over their city, but also of the recent things that had been happening. "That sounds familiar. Unfortunately, a bit more familiar than you can imagine."

"How so?" Julianne responded.

Taking a deep breath, Amelia said, "To keep a *very* long story short, I accidentally hired Adrien's bastard daughter to be the Dean of Students. More than that, she has what I could only describe as a dark mystic in her employ. I don't know if she's one of your New Dawn people, but Scarlett is definitely up to no good."

Julianne's eyes widened, unable to believe what she was hearing. Was it possible this Scarlett was one of them? One of the New Dawn? The name didn't sound familiar to Julianne, but that didn't necessarily mean that she didn't know her. The rogue mystic could have changed it, or she may have been at the Temple before Julianne had met her.

Their situations seemed so much different until then. It was possible they both faced the same enemy, but she had no way of knowing for sure without a little digging. Julianne's eyes flashed white as she dipped into Amelia's mind. It was obvious the Chancellor knew it was happening, but she allowed the intrusion with no protest.

When she was finished looking, her eyes returned to normal. "This Scarlett person is unfamiliar to me, but that doesn't mean anything. I know nothing of the New Dawn yet. It's possible she is self-taught, or perhaps she left the Temple before I met her."

"How much of a threat do they pose?" Amelia asked.

Julianne shifted in her chair. "They've managed to find some way of shielding that can't be penetrated, so I can't be sure. It seems they hail from the other side of the Madlands, which is where I'm headed now."

She sighed, shaking her head. They'd fought together before, and she wished she could stay and help now, but with so many lives on the line in the Temple—*her* people's lives—she couldn't pull away from her mission.

Finally, she said, "I wish I could stay to help you. I feel compelled to, but I have a responsibility to my people, and they atta—"

"No, no, no," Amelia said, reaching over to give Julianne's hand a light squeeze. "Don't do that. You don't have to make excuses to me. You always belonged in the Heights, and I belong here. We worked together to free the city, but we have our responsibilities to our homes. I know you'd stay if you could. *I* would go with *you* if I could, but my city is in danger, and I can't leave. I truly understand. Seems we have our own paths to take."

Julianne smiled, but it was forced. It hurt her deeply not to be able to help her friend.

Amelia sighed. "Still, I can't help but ask. Are you sure that's a good idea? Going to the Madlands, I mean. If something happened to you out there—"

"The Temple would have all the resources it needs to carry on without me. I've planned for the worst, though I certainly hope it doesn't come to that."

"I see." Amelia gazed over steepled fingers. "If there's anything I can do to help, I will. Our resources are thin, and I'm stuck here, but I'll commit what I can."

Smiling, Julianne said, "No, there's no need. I only came to warn you of their presence, but it seems like you may have already been aware of it. Of the six that came to us, only three remain. I assume those three are the ones that attacked us on the mountain."

Amelia gasped. "Attacked?"

"Yes. We almost lost someone, not from our party but known to our rearick. I couldn't leave without telling you. Actually, could you spare a messenger? I need to let my people know what happened."

Swallowing hard, Amelia nodded. "Of course. I only have a very few trusted guards, Marcus among them, though I've had him buried in responsibility training the new Guard recruits. I'll brief those who need to know and perhaps put some feelers out for more information if I can. You're sure there's nothing else I can do to help?"

Resolutely, Julianne shook her head. She could see Amelia was stretched thin already.

Amelia nodded. "Very well. Please let me know if that changes. I'll send a trusted courier to your room at the inn tomorrow morning to take your message. I wish you all a safe journey and a fast return. Stay safe, Julianne. Irth needs you."

Amelia showed Julianne to the door. They hugged briefly, and Julianne stepped outside, the lock behind her clicking shut after a moment.

"And where has my intrepid protector gone, I wonder?" Julianne murmured to herself. She rounded a corner and caught sight of Garrett, leaning against a wall, deep in conversation. She froze, recognizing that blonde hair and easy posture anywhere.

"Oh, aye, there she is now," Garrett said, gesturing her over. "Look what I found rolling 'round the hallways of the Chancellor's office."

"Hello, Marcus," Julianne said, using a meditative trick to slow down her suddenly racing heart.

"Julianne!" Marcus grinned widely. "I see you're off on another adventure? And what on Irth happened to your face?"

"Just a mishap," she said, shooting Garrett a quick look. He shrugged.

"Oh, he didn't tell me anything. I just hadn't expected to see you outside of the Heights again so soon. Are you heading back, or will you stay a few days? Perhaps we can catch up while you're here."

A hopeful lilt to his voice made Garrett snort. He raised his hands in defense when Marcus shot out a foot to kick him in the ankle. "Well, perhaps the young guardsman here will offer to escort the lady back to her accommodation? If so, I have me own business to tend to while we're here."

"It's almost midnight," Julianne snapped. "What the hell kind of business could you have *now*?"

"Well, it mostly involves a soft pillow and a lack of opportunity to stick me boot in me mouth, to be honest. If I may?"

Unable to outright forbid him from leaving, Julianne nodded. "We leave early. Be ready."

"Aye, lass. Farewell, Marcus. Try not to get stabbed before I see ye next."

"You, too, rearick." Marcus waved as Garrett sauntered away, then turned to Julianne. "You're going home already?"

"No," she admitted. "I'll be away for a while, actually. I'm looking for someone, a mystic who was last seen across the Madlands."

Marcus let out a low whistle. "Jules, that's not a trip to take lightly."

She raised her eyebrows at him.

"I know you know it's risky. I was just surprised, that's all. Especially because I'm headed the same way," he said.

Suspicious, Julianne narrowed her eyes. "Really."

Marcus grinned. "Really. I miss it, crazy as it sounds. Plus, we had a remnant attack not long ago. I figured it wouldn't hurt to go spy around and make sure they stay there in the Madlands while I find my own path. Since Amelia took over, the city has been getting much better. I like it here and all, but it's so… *boring.*"

"Shouldn't that be a good thing?" Julianne asked. "And aren't you needed with all the things going on right now?"

"It *is* a good thing, really, and I know Amelia needs me, but I think I could be of better use out there. Even with everything going on, I think the people are safer now than ever." Marcus shrugged. "I planned to head out to the border, see if I could pick up some work there, maybe find a small travelling party who are moving through. I spent so long fighting out there and never saw what's on the other side."

"Probably more of the same," Julianne said. "People, towns."

"Probably." Still wearing that ridiculously charming smile, Marcus tapped his chin with one finger. "I have to go. Gotta make sure a bunch of whiny recruits are hitting the sheets. I wake 'em up good and early. Take care, will you? I don't want you to get eaten out there."

"I'll be fine. Garrett's coming, and we both know he can fight. Others, too," she added, once again feeling the chafe of her solitary journey becoming a group venture. "Farewell, Marcus."

Marcus hesitated, then darted in and brushed his lips against her cheek. She flushed, but before she could find her tongue, he was walking away.

Pressing a hand to her sternum to recenter herself, Julianne hurried away. It was late, and she would need to catch as much rest as she could before setting off in the morning.

CHAPTER EIGHTEEN

A tap on the bedroom door woke Julianne with a start. The few snatched hours of restless sleep had made even her dreams tense and she jerked awake, then relaxed as she realized it was just the innkeeper, waking them as requested.

Rolling out of bed, Julianne pulled her riding dress over her petticoat. Throwing the few belongings she'd unpacked back into her bag, she nudged Bette.

"Time to go," she whispered.

Bette sat up, then threw her legs over the side of her bed, inserting them straight into a pair of boots. She stood, stretched, and slung her pack over one shoulder before walking to the door.

"What, that's it?" Julianne asked, wrapping the leather cord around her boots. "And I thought *I* was low maintenance." She stood and slipped on her white robe.

"It comes with practice," Bette admitted.

Julianne slipped into a light trance. She reached out to give Danil and Bastian a sharp nudge, but couldn't help but notice Bette's quiet pride at Julianne's remark. It made the mystic smile.

Bette had been a pleasure to ride with, and was quick witted to boot. Julianne had a hunch that Bette's presence would take some of the edge off of travelling with so many.

A thud sounded through the wall, and then came a grumbled curse. "Bitch's oath, they're loud."

Julianne chuckled. "That they are. Come on, let's wait downstairs. By the sound of it, we'll be lucky if they don't come out with their trousers on their heads instead of their backsides."

Bette barked a loud laugh, then slapped a hand over her mouth. The two slipped down the narrow staircase and outside, whispering thanks to the innkeeper as she stoked the fire for the morning meal.

It wasn't long before the courier showed to take her message —just as Amelia had promised. She'd quickly scrawled it the night before, a hurried explanation of their encounter on the mountain and a warning to stay safe.

Stamping her feet to ward off the cold, Julianne waited for the others and sent Bette to start readying the horses. Bette returned only a moment later with a stable boy, leading all five horses between them.

"The innkeep planned ahead and made sure our horses were ready," Bette explained.

"Ahh, thank goodness for small favors." Julianne patted her mare's neck, snuggling in to share the warmth.

The door opened and Garrett tumbled out alongside Bastian. Though Garrett was dressed and ready, Bastian's pack still hung open as he struggled to drag his robes on, boots in one hand.

"Here," Julianne said. "Let me help." She took Bastian's pack, then tugged the robe on properly. He gave a thankful smile and sat to pull his boots on, almost tripping Danil in the doorway.

"Oops, sorry." Danil said. "Jules, you should have woken us sooner."

"How am I supposed to wake you while I'm still asleep? You lot had just as long as we did to get ready. It's not our fault you're slow. You're like a couple of teenage girls."

"What did I say?" Bette remarked dryly, causing a burst of giggles from Julianne. "Here, take yer horse, Garrett."

He did so, mounting quickly and moving away so the others had room to do the same. By the time they were on their way, the sun was just cresting the horizon.

Did your meeting with Amelia go well? Danil sent as they walked their horses to the city gate.

As well as could be expected. It seems the Arcadians have some issues of their own, but Amelia is strong. I have faith in her, she replied.

Do you think... Danil's thoughts trailed off as something caught his attention. His face hardened. *Someone's waiting for us at the gate.*

Julianne quickly reached out with her mind, then jerked her reins as she recognized the slim shadow on his horse by the exit to Arcadia.

"Marcus! What are ye doing out so bloody early?" Garrett called.

Butterflies danced in Julianne's stomach. She knew exactly what he was doing.

"When I heard a party was headed for the Madlands, how could I not? I've been itching to return for months." Marcus moved his horse forwards and bowed a greeting. "I spent years fighting at the border. Never once did I see the other side of it. I figured, now's as good a time as any. If you'll have me, of course."

Julianne started to tell him no, that their party was full and they couldn't possibly accommodate another, but she was cut off before she even had the chance to begin.

"That'd be just about perfect," Garrett said. "Old Harker never meant to only send the two of us as guards, but what with all the last-minute changes, we couldn't find an extra body."

"And who's paying for this extra body?" Julianne demanded. "I've already doubled my hire fee and paid an arm and a leg for the booking." She prayed Marcus would take the hint.

"Oh, you don't need to pay me. Like I said, I was going to head this way eventually, even if I had to go alone." Marcus grinned, then waited for Julianne's answer. Though his demeanor was nonchalant, she could feel his bated breath and his anxious hope that she would say yes.

She crumbled. Logic be damned, and bad ideas, too. She *wanted* him to come. "Fine. You've got your own supplies?" she asked.

"Sure do. I'm armed to the teeth, too. You won't get through the Madlands without some magitech. Adrien was a dick, but he left behind some really nice stuff."

"If you're gonna brag about it, you'd better be sharing," Garrett said.

"Of course! I'd never let a friend carry an inferior weapon." Marcus winked and Garrett cracked up.

Julianne just rolled her eyes.

Marcus guided his horse so it fell in beside her as the party of six left the city. "I'm sorry. I put you on the spot, I know."

"Bullshit. You're not sorry; you planned that down to the minute," she murmured to him.

He shrugged. "Guilty as charged."

Julianne glanced away, only to catch Danil's eye. Her heart sank when she realized, for the first time, he'd completely blocked her from his mind. Pain lanced her chest, and she looked away, staring at the road, lips pressed tightly together.

What had she been thinking?

It's fine, really, Danil sent. *Don't worry about me.*

Danil...

I just need a bit of time.

Cursing, Julianne nudged her horse ahead to ride lead with Bette, who'd taken Garrett's place from the day before.

"What do you think—" Bette started, then caught sight of Julianne's face. "What's wrong?"

Julianne winced. It was unlike her to let her emotions be so visibly on display. As the leader of a group of people who could read minds, she'd long since mastered the art of calmness. Now, however, she was away from the safety and familiarity of the Temple, and dealing with emotions that were otherwise quite foreign to her.

"Just… men," was all Julianne offered.

"Oh, aye. That pretty one?"

Julianne didn't have to delve into Bette's mind to confirm she meant Marcus. He *was* pretty, with those big brown eyes and floppy hair. His smile was contagious, and not just to women. Marcus had an easy air about him that made him easy to be friends with and invoked a feeling of trust.

"Aye," Julianne said, shooting Bette a grateful glance.

"I suppose it's a bit awkward, what with Danil mooning over ye. D'ye think anything will happen with either of them?"

"No. Maybe. Oh, hell, I don't know." She didn't want to think about it either.

"Well, if ye ask my advice, and ye should, I say make 'em both wait until ye know yer own heart. As long as ye do that, everything will work out." Bette gave Julianne a reassuring grin.

"That's very good advice, Bette."

Conversation ceased as they reached the farmlands surrounding the city. They rode the horses harder there, setting a steady pace that would—with luck—hold over the next few days.

The grassy hoofbeats and sharp breeze made casual conversation difficult, which suited Julianne. She didn't reach out mentally, except to occasionally check on their party. Instead, she concentrated on the ride, making sure she sat the horse well and wasn't wearing the animal down.

They reached a stream when the sun was at its peak, and a brief discussion led to the decision to stop for lunch. Julianne nibbled at a strip of jerky while her horse pulled at the long grass by the water.

"What's her name?" Bette asked, catching Julianne staring at the horses.

"Whose name?"

"The horse." Bette's eyebrows shot up when Julianne shrugged. "What? How can a pretty beast like that not have a name?"

"I don't know. It never occurred to me. She's just a horse, after all."

"Bloody mystics." Bette threw her hands up in the air. "Ye spend all yer time with feelin' and thought, and never once spare one fer yer animals. I'm not goin' another step until that horse has a name."

"Gertrude," Julianne said immediately.

"A *pretty* name." Bette rolled her eyes. "Like Stardust, for the white smatter across her flank. Or Lightning, though she's not overly fast. Hmm. It needs to be a gentle name, but one that's strong."

Julianne regarded the horse with skepticism. The mare continued to pull at weeds, looking unperturbed by her lack of a name. Still, Bette seemed insistent. The white patch under the horse's belly merged with the patchy grey of her coat. "Cloud Dancer?" Julianne suggested.

"Perfect. You watch, she'll be a right friend to ye now." Bette stuffed the last of her bread into her mouth, then stood. "That's enough lollygagging. We'd best be off, before we lose too much time."

Garrett hoisted a groaning Bastian to his feet. "Give it a few days, lad. Yer ass'll toughen up."

"Not before it falls off," Bastian muttered.

"Come on, don't want to let the ladies show us up, eh?" Marcus winked at Bastian as he sprang onto his horse.

Bastian ignored him. He rankled at the new addition to their party, and seethed at the disrespect the guard had shown Master Julianne. He'd seen flashes of their previous encounter in Marcus's mind—Julianne and Danil had both been locked down tightly since Marcus had joined them—and though nothing had happened then, Marcus had felt Julianne was interested in him.

Bastian stifled a snort as he pulled himself up on his horse. Julianne would never associate with someone like that. The man didn't have an ounce of class.

Gritting his teeth, Bastian guided his horse to the middle of the line. Once they were moving steadily, he slipped into a light meditation to numb the pain in his legs.

By the time they reached the Madlands, three days on a horse had both helped and hindered Bastian's efforts in the saddle. His muscles were slowly adjusting and his posture had improved, but the relentless travel drained him of all enthusiasm for the journey. He was tired, crabby, and sore from head to toe, not to mention covered in grime.

The young mystic, lost in desperate meditation, didn't notice the changing in the air until the horses stopped.

"No place like home," Marcus said. He drew a deep breath in through his nose, wrinkling it at the acrid scent. He slipped off his horse and patted her neck, then tied her to a straggling branch. "We rest, now. Spend the night here and set off into the Madlands fresh and rested.

"But—" Julianne's disagreement was cut off before it was voiced.

"Nay, lass. He's right. The Madlands is not a place to wander into tired and unprepared," Garrett said.

Julianne considered for a moment, then nodded. Marcus was already half unpacked, with his saddlebags open and a small lean-to on the ground beside him.

"Even here, I want eyes watching through the night. If one of those bastards wanders too far, it'll be on us without warning. I'll take first watch, Garrett the second. Bette can round out the remaining hours while the rest of you get some sleep."

"I'd offer to take a turn, but…" Danil shrugged one shoulder and grinned. "Don't think I'd be much use."

"Uhh… I could take a watch. If you need me to, I mean." Bastian looked thoroughly displeased at the idea.

"No, you rest. Tomorrow night will be different, double guard, all night. Enjoy it while you can." Marcus smiled to take any sting out of his words, and threw his pack on the ground. "No fire tonight, or any night while we're in the hot spot."

Julianne shivered at the thought of sleeping without a heat source. She, Bastian and Danil could make themselves comfortable through meditation, but the others would have to suffer the chill. If it got too cold, no mind trick would stop the reality of frostbite.

They set up camp before nightfall, then sat and talked, voices low and conversation sparse. The looming presence of the Madlands stifled the group's usual banter, and each small noise smothered the group in silence as they wondered what it might be.

As soon as the sun dropped below the mountains, Julianne crawled into her bed, Bette following behind.

"You lot should go to sleep, too. Garrett, I'll wake you when it's time?" Marcus whispered.

"Aye. Just give me blankets a good kick, and I'll be up."

Bastian, Danil, and Garrett soon left for bed, leaving Marcus alone in the dark. He stood, stretching his tender muscles.

Too damn long in that town, he thought.

He wasn't lying when he said he was itching to get back out here. He'd been part of a group that guarded the border between the Madlands and Arcadia.

They'd killed any remnant that came close to crossing over, and it seemed they'd done their job well. The incursions reduced, forcing the guards to go days without seeing action or, more likely, sending them into the hot zone to find it.

Marcus hated cities. Too crowded and close, with the stink of other people all around. Here? Clean air, fresh water, and the chance to swing a weapon once in a while. Oh, sure, it was dangerous—but so was walking through the streets of Arcadia at night. Marcus much preferred to face off with a slavering beast than with a man who'd just made a bad choice.

He walked the perimeter of their tiny camp, watching for any sign of movement in the darkness—not that it would help. He knew he'd hear the remnant before he saw them. Sneaking wasn't one of their strong suits.

A rustle in the bushes made Marcus pause in his circuit, heart in his mouth, muscles ready to spring into action. A squirrel darted out from a bush, and he immediately relaxed. It scampered past the tents, stopping twice to sniff the air before racing off into the darkness.

When the moon dipped close to the tree line, Marcus gave Garrett a gentle nudge with the toe of his boot. When the rearick didn't budge, he nudged harder. The third time was a solid kick, causing Garrett to choke on a snore and sit bolt upright, hand on the sword he'd left next to his bedroll.

"Shh. It's your shift," Marcus whispered.

"Aye. Right. Erm…" Garrett shook his head roughly, then looked up with clear eyes and a grin. "Right then! Off to bed with ye."

Marcus lay down, thankful he hadn't had to endure another night of the rearick's thunderous snoring. As he rolled over to sleep, his thoughts drifted away from issues of safety and preparedness to the girl lying just a few feet away in another tent.

CHAPTER NINETEEN

Dawn broke with a fight between two angry birds. The cacophony brought everyone out, Bette cursing the feathered foes while Danil laughed at Bastian who was shaking his fist at them.

Julianne sucked in a deep breath. The air was different here. Some tinge to the freshness, an odor she wasn't used to. It wasn't strong enough to put a finger on it, but it was there. The mystic quickly performed her morning meditations, then readied herself to go. Marcus slipped up beside her as she was fastening the saddlebags on her horse.

The weapon in his hand was one she'd seen before, a magitech device that would cause serious damage to anyone he used it against. Julianne wasn't exactly sure how it worked, but she was reassured by the confidence with which he carried it.

"You're sure you know what you're in for out there?" he asked quietly.

Julianne nodded. "I've heard the stories, seen some things." She didn't mention the 'things' she'd seen were from his own mind—memories of hard fights, sparse rations, and adrenalin-filled hunts for the scavenging beasts of the Madlands.

"If you're still sure you want to do this… we travel fast." He glanced around as though already on the lookout for danger. "Don't split up, ever, not for any reason. A larger party will work against us, but the benefit in numbers still applies. Besides, I don't trust anyone here to lead a group all the way through, except maybe Garrett. If he died, whoever was with him would go down like a stone."

Julianne blanched, but he continued. "If someone is left behind, they're dead, so no one gets left behind unless they already are. No fires; no loud noises. No hunting, either. I swear those bastards can smell fresh blood from a mile away. If we get caught out, end up in a bad place, we sacrifice a horse. Or all of them, if that's what it takes." He watched Julianne's face as it drained of blood. Her chin twitched, just the tiniest bit, and she pressed her lips together.

Then, she nodded curtly. "Thank you, Marcus. I'm glad you're with us."

He grinned. "You don't shake easily, do you?"

It was Julianne's turn to smile. "If I recall, it was you doing the shaking when we were in the Frozen North." They'd travelled together when she was masquerading as Stellan, one of Adrien's guards, during the rebellion in Arcadia.

They had trekked through bad weather, two strangers with little trust between them, Marcus working for the people Julianne had been working against. Though she'd told him how close she'd been to pushing him off a high ledge at the time, she didn't think he really believed it.

With a wink, she turned away and put one foot in a stirrup. "Hurry up. Just because no one gets left behind doesn't mean we'll wait all day for you, soldier."

Barking a laugh, Marcus strode back over to the campsite. Julianne watched as he kicked dirt and leaves about, covering the signs they'd camped there. He then checked that the rest of the team was ready to go.

When he approached Bastian, he pulled something out of his pocket. Julianne didn't recognize the device, but figured it was magitech when she glimpsed the small glowing stone set into the side.

Marcus leaned his head close to Bastian, probably discussing how it worked. When Marcus stepped back, Bastian lifted it up.

A hollow thud sounded, and the tree in front of Bastian shook, shards of bark scattering into the air as a chunk exploded. The big tree still stood, but it looked like someone had cleaved a messy chunk out of it with a giant axe.

"Just like that," Marcus said. "It may not take a man out in one shot, and it takes a moment to recharge, but that'll buy me time to save your ass in a fight."

"Seriously?" Bastian asked. "With one of these, it'll be me saving *your* ass." He pocketed the device as Marcus laughed.

"I'd lay money on you blowing your own balls off before that happens. Besides, these are no good—" Marcus patted his own weapon, a long, staff-like piece of magitech "—unless you know how to fight. Not just lay down a punch or shoot a weapon, but *fight*. Anticipate. Predict. Plan."

Bastian took the friendly warning for what it was, self-consciously adjusting himself as he grimaced at the bulge in his pocket where the weapon sat. After a moment's thought, he pulled it out and tossed it in his pack. Garrett laughed behind him, but the young mystic didn't seem fazed by the teasing.

Despite the change in plans, she *was* glad to have Marcus with them, and not just for the weapons he'd brought. Taking Danil into the Madlands worried her. As helpful and kind hearted as he was, not to mention as proficient back at the Temple, she knew his disability was a liability out here. Having Bastian along as well worried her even more.

They wove down into the valley in a single file. The trees down here were a different species from those that grew through most of Irth. Stark, white trunks stretched so far overhead they couldn't see the tips, while branches spread out to the sides and dropped pine-scented needles to the forest floor.

Julianne reached out and trailed her fingers along a nearby branch. She sniffed it gingerly, and screwed up her face. Yes, it was the trees that smelled. Instead of fresh and clean, the pine here had a sharp, coppery odor.

"They say the smell is from all the blood the trees have soaked up, remnant and our people alike," Marcus called from behind.

"Every place has its ghost story." Julianne glanced over her shoulder, but quickly jerked her head back as her horse nosed around a bend in the trail. "Is it all like this?" she asked.

"No," Marcus replied. "Just wait. You'll see."

He wouldn't elaborate, and Julianne let him have his secrets. Delving into his mind during this part of the journey would be foolhardy. She needed every ounce of concentration she had to navigate her horse down the winding path and keep her from placing a foot wrong on the twisted roots below. Finally, the forest thinned out, and Julianne gaped at the sight before her.

The trail emerged into a valley scattered with old ruins. Buildings jutted out of the low-lying greenery. Some had crumbled to almost nothing, others stood tall in some semblance of the dignity they'd once had. Vines and creepers snuck through cracks and chasms, and trees stretched up from windows turned askew by failing foundations.

Julianne shuddered as she wondered what Arcadia or even the Temple would look like decades after the humans had left.

"What's that?" Bastian sent Julianne the image of what he was seeing, and she swung her head around to look. By the path ahead, a sculpture of twisted metal jutted out of the thick trunk of a tree.

"Ancient ruins," Marcus explained. "My old commander said the tree must have grown into the metal, and around it."

Julianne rode past slowly, unable to tear her eyes away from it. It wasn't until a gasp from Bette that she focused on what lay ahead.

"What in the Bitch's name is that thing?" Bette had stopped, heedless of Garrett almost plowing into her.

"What yer… oh! Well, that's a damn sight." Garrett craned his head back, and Julianne jumped into his mind to get a better look.

Ahead, a tall building, crumbled away on one side, sparkled in the early morning sun. Clean surfaces reflected the daylight, sending scattered sparkles over the ground

"A sight she is, alright," Marcus murmured. He'd moved up beside Julianne, but when she cleared her vision and glanced over at him, he was staring at her. He quickly looked away, smothering a small smile. "A nest of remnant used to live in the lower levels. We'll get a good look, but not up close. My unit cleared them out of there twice, but there's no telling if they've returned."

"How does it sparkle?" Julianne asked as they moved on.

"Not sure what it's made of. Some kind of glass maybe? I don't see how glass could hold up a whole building, but the ancients did a lot of weird stuff like that." Marcus ushered them along, reluctant to stop.

"Maybe it's just a coating?" Bastian suggested, craning his neck as his horse ambled on, oblivious to the wonders around them.

"Maybe. The lower levels are covered in plant growth, but for some reason it never really climbed to the top. Too slippery, maybe. There's some mold coating the higher levels, but it grows in clumps and washes away in heavy rain, leaving it… well, like that." Marcus craned his neck to take in the massive structure.

Julianne thought back to the storm that had hit the Temple the night Donna had shown up. Strange, how one little weather event could not only accompany such disaster, but create such beauty.

Deeper in the valley, more crumbling walls appeared. The

paths between them were strangely flat, as though the roots of more substantial trees couldn't penetrate the ground. They rode quietly, not speaking, through the warped shadows of a city long forgotten by its people.

Julianne's skin crawled even as she admired the beauty. Sunlight sparkled through leaves, touching old stone and rusted, metal carcasses. Overhead, a crow called, the only sign of wildlife they'd seen since beginning their descent.

"Come on, you lot," Danil said nervously. "Kind of hard to see where I'm going with you all jumping at shadows. You're all giving me the creeps."

"Toughen up, lad," Garrett said, his voice wobbly.

"Me?" Forgetting himself, Danil's voice carried loudly, bouncing off the structures around them. "You're the worst of them all."

"Hush," Julianne admonished.

"Easy for you to say," Danil muttered. "You're stone cold, Jules. How are you not crapping your pants down here?"

She laughed nervously. "I am. I'm just doing it behind a damn good shield."

Danil blew out a breath, trying to shake off the oppressive sense of danger that leaked through the shadows around them. Marcus led them through the old city, steering them away from more substantial buildings in favor of those that had worn away almost to nothing.

They reached an open area, and Marcus nudged them on faster. "Come on. Sooner we're out of this place, the better."

"Why? Won't it be worse—" Julianne cut off with a scream as something skittered through the leaves, sending her horse into a terrified frenzy. It reared up, then struck the ground with its hooves. The crunch echoed loudly as the other horses whinnied and danced.

Then, the city swallowed them.

The ground split apart, and rocks tumbled into the dark

cavern as the horses scrambled for purchase on the sliding stone ground.

Julianne heard someone scream, but she wasn't sure who. She gripped her horse but couldn't hold on and when they fell, Cloud Dancer skidded and toppled, landing on her mistress as the dust settled. The horse kicked and jerked, and her great head connected with Julianne's skull.

A light above bobbed, flickered, and went out.

CHAPTER TWENTY

Jules? Jules, you need to wake up. Now, Jules. You don't have time to rest. Jules, wake up, Jules.

Go away! She mentally shouted the words even as consciousness returned. Julianne sucked in a breath, then coughed out a lungful of dust as needles of pain stabbed at her head.

Hands helped her to sit. "It's ok, Jules. I'm sorry. You needed to wake up." Danil's voice murmured in her ear, voice soothing as his thoughts inside her head were not.

She briefly felt his weight in her mind, checking she was coherent and remembered the moments before the impact.

Danil's prodding was standard protocol—after a concussion, a person needed rest, but could be woken if it wasn't safe to do so. Julianne would pay for it later, but for now, the ache in her head was bearable and they needed to get out of here, wherever 'here' was.

"Everyone ok?" she asked, voice hoarse. She blinked the grit from her eyes and found she could see. Light filtered through a hole above their heads, though her eyes didn't want to adjust enough to see into the surrounding shadows.

"Looks like we all survived. Horses are all standing, but we won't know if they're lame until we get out of this hole." Garrett plunged into the shadows. "What is this place?"

"Some kind of ancient, underground building." Marcus kicked at some rubbish by his feet. "I've heard tales of them, but never seen one."

Danil helped Julianne to stand, letting go once she'd assured him her balance was fine. She picked her way over the fallen stone from above and looked around the cavernous space.

Dust coated every surface, obscuring any clue as to what the area once served as. Shadows in the dark corners outlined benches, and the floor was scattered with smaller objects. Julianne kneeled down to inspect one.

She picked it up and rolled it in her hand. It was cold and round, with blunt ends.

"What's that?" Bastian's sudden question startled her and she dropped her prize. It smashed, shattering on the hard floor and splashing putrid liquid all over her skirt.

"Shit." A foul odor reached Julianne's nose. "Ugh, that smell is hideous." She backed away and found Marcus pulling things from a wall.

"Might have been food. Maybe this was a storehouse of some kind." He shook the box in his hand and it rustled. "Either way, we need to get moving. The noise from the cave-in probably attracted attention, and we don't want to be fighting from the lower ground if we can help it."

A quick examination showed that the roof had fallen in such a way that the horses, if led carefully, should be able to climb out.

"We risk hurting them more, dragging them up that rubbish," Bette pointed out.

"If we leave them here, they'll end up dinner for a local remnant pack," Marcus said.

Bette shuddered and grabbed her horse's halter. "Best be quick about it, then."

The beasts seemed as eager to leave the eerie, forgotten room as their riders did. Within a short time, all six of them stood in the bright sunlight again beside the hole from the cave-in.

Marcus reached up to grasp the pommel of his saddle. Then, all hell broke loose.

Julianne stifled a scream as two remnant descended on them.

"Dinner coming to us tonight?" a voice growled as they sprang out from behind a shattered wall.

The rag-clad men dove towards them wielding heavy, barbed clubs. Julianne yanked Bastian backwards, just in time for a weapon to go sailing past his nose.

His horse screamed and reared up, smashing the remnant with her hooves. The feral man dove to the ground and stabbed up with his spear, heedless of the frantic animal trying to clobber him to death.

Julianne ripped her short walking staff free from her pack and stabbed it forwards. Her target skittered backwards, out of reach, then lunged forwards to grab the end of it. Julianne's guard training took over, and she whipped it out of reach, then swung it back to connect with the remnant's bony ribs.

"Behind!" Garrett hollered as Marcus stepped in front of her.

The young soldier swung his weapon upwards, and the remnant jerked back, guts spilling onto the ground. The beast's mouth hung open as he stared, eyes wide, before crumbling to the ground.

Retching from a smell so much worse than what had soaked her dress, Julianne almost missed the next attack. A remnant launched for Marcus, whose weapon was still recharging. He whipped a knife up, slicing the remnant's belly open. Snapping up with his fist, he then stabbed at the beast's throat. The remnant collapsed in a gurgle of bloody bubbles.

In the few seconds Marcus had taken to fight, more had appeared. Garrett and Bette circled a remnant that was armed with a short sword. Another crept towards Danil from behind.

Danil caught the view in Julianne's mind and dropped to the

ground as it swung for his head. He rolled on his back and kicked, his legs caught in his traditional robes. Julianne dove for them, cracked her staff over the remnant's head hard enough to make the wood tremble in her hands.

It didn't fall. If anything, the attack enraged it, sending it into a frenzy. A frenzy directed at Julianne. It stared her down, mucous gathered in one corner of its eye, blistering pustules weeping around it. It took a step towards her. She took one back, fumbling at her belt for the small knife she carried.

"Bitch. You die!"

CHAPTER TWENTY-ONE

It leapt. The frail, scabbed body pressed against Julianne as it gnashed its teeth, trying to bite her face. Teeth sank into her arm and she screamed, slashing forwards with her tiny weapon.

"You'll make a nice dinner, bitch," the remnant spat, Julianne's blood on its chin.

"This dinner bites back," she said through bared teeth.

Julianne stabbed an eye, the sickening pop almost as awful as the clear fluid that ran down and splashed her face. The remnant didn't react, except to struggle harder against the arm Julianne had thrown up to protect her vulnerable throat.

Jerking the knife free she thrust again, piercing the side of the face, then again at the ear. This time, she hit her mark, shoving the blade deep into the creature's head.

It spasmed.

"Dinner bitch… bites." Coughing once, a barrage of chunky saliva and mucous coming along with it, the beast collapsed on top of her, the dead weight squeezing the breath from her lungs.

Heaving, Julianne kicked and shoved until the body rolled off.

Julianne forced herself up to her knees, shaking. She looked up to see Marcus kicking the fallen body of a remnant. Bette and

Garrett were wiping their weapons clean and Bastian stood, staring at his Master, face pale and body trembling.

"Bitch's britches, Jules. I know you learned to fight a bit in Arcadia, but I didn't know you could do *that*." Danil's eyes were as wide as Bastian's.

"We—I should have helped. I'm sorry, Master, I didn't—" Bastian began.

Julianne cut off Bastian's stammered apology. "You weren't trained for this. None of us were, really. That's why we brought them." She jerked her head at Marcus and the rearick. The soldier dipped his head with a wry smile.

"She's right." Marcus stepped forwards smoothly, taking Bastian's shoulders. "But perhaps we should change that before we go too much further. I can't teach you to fight, but I can give you some basic skills to give you half a chance." He looked down at Julianne's soiled clothes and wrinkled his nose. "With any luck, that stink will scare away anything else till we get through the city proper."

"I'm half tempted to strip it off and leave it," she said without thinking.

"I never thought I'd see *him* speechless," Garrett said with a snigger. Julianne looked at Marcus, realizing what she'd said.

He was red, lips pressed together as he tried to restrain himself. He failed, bursting into laughter that wasn't at all muffled by the fist he shoved in his mouth.

"Is it safer once we pass through?" Danil asked when Marcus had himself under control. The blind mystic smothered a grin, but didn't comment on Julianne's proposal.

"Aye," Bette spoke up. "That is, if what I heard was correct?"

Marcus nodded an affirmative. "Come on. Sorry, Jules, no time to stop. You'll just have to keep your clothes on… but maybe walk downwind of the rest of us?" He winked, ignoring her furious scowl. "Once we're far enough away from this mess we can stop to regroup, but we'll be in remnant territory for a few days."

Julianne looked at her horse. Cloud Dancer seemed to sense her intent and shuffled away. Julianne gently pulled her harness until she was eye to eye with the beast. "Listen here, horse. I don't like this any more than you do, but Bitch be damned if I'm going to extend this any longer by going on foot."

Cloud Dancer snorted and rolled her eyes.

Bette stepped up to her. "Aye, pretty Cloud. Don't ye listen to this one. Now, you be a good pony and let the Master hop up, aye?" Bette patted the horse's nose and Julianne took the opportunity to mount up. The horse tensed, but allowed her to keep her seat.

"I told ye," Bette lectured, "She needs a name, and ye need to use it. She'll be much more polite if ye do."

Julianne rolled her eyes, trying not to wonder if she looked like Cloud Dancer while doing it. She nudged the horse with her knees and the party set off, now trying to avoid both large, empty areas and the dense greenery at the edges of the roads.

"The sooner we're out of this bloody ghost city, the better," Garrett mumbled.

By mid-afternoon, the cluster of tumbled-down buildings had turned into twisted forest with only occasional broken stones and rusted metal bars as evidence people had once lived there. They passed two abandoned hovels, evidenced by dried, chewed bones and burnt out campfires. Other things, like trinkets and fabric scraps scattered the areas, lying tossed aside with little care.

Julianne nursed her aching head, avoiding magic use for now. It hadn't even occurred to her to use it during the attack—not just because of the sudden appearance of the remnant, but because she'd always been told they were like animals.

Mental magic only worked on humans, unlike druidic magic, which worked on animals and not people. Remnant were somewhere in between, descended from human ancestors who were lost to the madness that swept the world.

The Founder stopped its spread, but couldn't save those already beyond redemption. Hence, the remnant were born. Julianne knew from notes in the Temple that mystics couldn't access a remnant mind like a human one, but those notes were old and disjointed and only contained the little knowledge that was gained by those mystics that were brave enough to enter the Madlands.

She thought on that. If Druids had been able to affect a remnant's mind, surely she'd have heard of it?

Academic curiosity didn't trump common sense. If the chance to find out first hand if she could enter a remnant's mind never came, she wouldn't complain. Still, if a crisis occurred and it was their only way out... Julianne shuddered.

Delving into someone's mind, seeing their thoughts and feelings, was a personal act. Living in the head of one of those beasts, even for a moment, was something she could do without.

How are you feeling? Danil interrupted her train of thought, bringing Julianne back to the present.

Fine, she replied. *Just a little sore.*

Is it safe to be moving about, Master? Bastian asked. *When I trained with Melody, she said waking a concussed person should only be done as a last resort. What if you relapse?*

It's ok, Julianne sent to him. She glanced over with a reassuring smile. *As you develop your skill in reaching into other minds, you grow to know your own better, too. You will learn your limits and recognize impairments with precision.*

"How long until we make camp?" Oblivious to the mental conversation going on around him, Garrett called from the back of the line to Marcus, at the front.

"Getting tired, old man?" Marcus asked.

"Just worried you children won't be able to work yerselves tomorrow if we push too hard today, whippersnapper," Garrett said in a high, scratchy voice, imitating an old man. "Back when I was a laddie, I had to walk fifteen miles in the snow with no shoes, just to drink the muddy water out of a chamberpot for breakfast."

Marcus laughed, a clear, unencumbered sound that bounced off the mountains and back into the valley. Despite his earlier admonitions to stay quiet, Julianne enjoyed the sound. A short glance from Danil sent that feeling skittering behind a wall and she gave herself a mental shake.

Bastian, do you think you can hold a trance while riding?

He could, and he did. Julianne joined him, though her experience meant she was able to still keep a part of her mind actively guiding her horse, and watching Bastian to make sure he was safe. She guided him into her mind, and through projected thoughts and sensations, showed him what it felt like in her head at that moment.

There was the gentle throb where she'd been knocked, but she drew him along those pain lines to demonstrate that no major damage had been inflicted. She let him push against her walls from the inside, testing their strength and resilience.

Bastian's mind was wide open to her, and though she didn't intend to pry, Julianne couldn't help but reflexively check on him. His anxiety at being away from the Temple combined with the attack by the remnant had shaken him badly, though he barely showed it. Surly stoicism seemed to be his M.O. when things were unsure.

Even with him this far into her mind, Julianne was able to cordon off certain thoughts and emotions of her own. Bastian noticed that, and reacted with admiration and not a little envy.

Just you wait. In a few years, you'll be rivalling me in your strength and experience.

Bastian blushed and withdrew from her mind. When he moved back to speak with Garrett, she slumped in relief.

You're pushing too hard, Danil admonished.

I know, she replied, *but the poor kid is terrified I'm about to drop dead.*

"Here, let me lead your horse. You rest." Danil stretched a hand out, then quickly cut off her protest. "As long as you've got your eyes open a crack, I'll be fine."

Julianne did as he suggested, handing over her reins and settling into her saddle. The light meditation soon turned into a deeper one, and her eyelids drooped until only a slit of light showed beneath them. Twice, Danil nudged her gently as they closed just a little too far.

When they finally stopped, it was all Julianne could do to pull herself down to the ground and stumble into the tent Bette quickly erected for them. With an appreciation only gained by absolute fatigue, Julianne collapsed onto her thin mattress and finally fell into a deep, dreamless sleep.

She woke the next morning with a crick in her back. Rubbing sleep-gritted eyes, she crawled out of the tent to find Garrett distributing oat biscuits for breakfast.

"Here, lass. We thought ye might be needing the extra sleep, so I filled yer water bag while ye slept. We're about to be off, though, so ye'd best get a wriggle on."

"Thanks, Garrett." She took a long swallow and washed the cold water around her fuzzy mouth. She'd missed out on a chance to change and wash in the trickling stream she could hear nearby, but there was no use dwelling on that.

"Jules!" Marcus trotted over when he saw her. He bent close, examining her face carefully. "That bruise on your face is healing well. How's that bump?" Gentle fingers touched her scalp as he felt for it, his touch somehow tender, yet clinical.

"I feel fine, Marcus." She mustered up a smile and realized she did, indeed, feel fine. Until he prodded the tender lump, anyway. "Ow! You pig-fingered bastard, it's not going to get better if you poke at it like that!"

"Sorry." He gave her a chagrined look. "Are you ok to ride out? I don't feel safe waiting in one spot for too long after sunrise."

Julianne nodded. They quickly tidied up the campsite, Marcus obliterating any sign they'd been there. Julianne pulled herself up onto Cloud Dancer's back and waited as Garrett finished loading his things.

A cool breeze tickled Julianne's arms and sent the hairs on her neck stiff. The sounds of the forest lulled, a momentary break in the rustling leaves and singing birds, a speck of time when everyone was still.

The silence was shattered by a scream. High and afraid, it broke through the party and made the horses shudder and dance. It cut off with a thud.

CHAPTER TWENTY-TWO

The scream pierced the air again, this time sounding of pain and desperation. "Over there!" Marcus yelled. They forced their horses through shrubbery and fallen branches and kicked them up a bare rock face.

There, on the ground by a cliff face that stretched to over half the height of the ancient trees, lay a woman. Tears streamed down her face as she cowered over a twisted leg. Julianne blanched at the sight of white bone jutting past blood and flesh. The girl flinched at their presence, then moaned again as pain shook her core.

"Is she…" Bette began.

"A remnant." Garrett spat on the ground and turned away.

"Ye canna just leave her there, ye beast."

"Fine!" Garrett turned and swung his sword, almost cleaving Danil in two as the mystic jumped between the girl and the weapon intended for her. She choked mid-shriek and whimpered, eyes wide as she stared at the people around her. "What the bloody hell are ye doing ye blind fool?"

"Please," Danil gasped. "Let me try to reach her."

Garrett gripped his weapon so tight his knuckles went white.

Then he gave it a shake and lowered it. "Ye damned fool." He turned away and headed in the direction of the path they'd left.

"Danil, you can't save her." Marcus took Danil's shoulder and gave it a shake. "Look at that leg, she'll never survive an injury like that. Not out here."

"I have to try, if only to give her a comfortable end." Danil turned his head in Julianne's direction. "Help me, Jules. Please, help me."

"Help me."

All eyes turned to the girl on the ground. Garrett spat again. "The wretches don't just speak. They think and they plan, too. Not like us, but enough to set a damn trap by shoving one of their own off a mountain." He eyed the cliff wall and the trees with distrust.

"Garrett's not wrong," Marcus said. He shifted, keeping a close eye on their surroundings. "Whatever you have to do, do it fast. Then, we go."

Julianne reached into Danil's mind. He was cut to the bone at the sight of the almost-human. Her bedraggled hair, crooked teeth and tear-swollen eyes had touched something in him. The certainty of her death weighed heavily on him, and he craved to ease her suffering before that happened if he could.

"Do it," she said. If it was a trap, she assumed, it would have already snapped closed. If Danil even had the smallest chance of reaching the remnant, so close to human and yet not, she had to know.

Danil pushed Julianne away as he prepared to try and direct his magic at the remnant. His usual spells used for seeing were released and his eyes cleared. The girl heaved and let out another yell, keening to the sky and gnashing her teeth, beside herself with pain. Julianne held her breath.

If anyone could do it, it would be Danil. His reliance on mind-reading to live his day to day life had given him unbeatable stamina and skill at penetrating difficult minds. Though Julianne was stronger as a whole, and more skilled, his single-minded practice was born of necessity and this gave him the edge.

His own mind-control skills were weak, but if he could link with the remnant, Julianne could use that as a conduit. Then, she would be able to twist the girl's comprehension of pain and give her a degree of comfort and peace before she left the world.

Danil's eyes turned white. Julianne watched as they fluttered. His knees bent and his back arched, then he flopped to the ground.

"Danil!" she screamed. "Danil, what is it?" She dove into his head and found only pain, hunger and fire. Teeth snapped at her and claws raked at her face and she cut the connection abruptly. Her face stung with scratches that didn't exist.

"Stop it, stop her!" Julianne desperately pointed at the girl, who lay writhing and gasping. Marcus walked over and raised his sword.

The remnant flinched back from the weapon, panting. Then, just before the blade sliced down, she jerked upright, baring the white, dirt-streaked skin of her throat.

With a single strike, he took her life. Both girl and mystic fell into stillness.

"Bitch and Bastard, Jules. Is he ok?"

"He's been... infected. Something is wrong with his mind," Bastian gasped. "It's like... like he's one of them." The boy's voice shook, and his pale skin betrayed the fear he couldn't voice.

Julianne pulled him to her in a fierce hug as Danil lay prone on the ground before her. "It'll be ok, Bastian. He'll be ok. He has to be..."

Julianne swallowed and braced herself. She tried to broach Danil's mind again. A growling wolf barred her way, baring its teeth when she tried to press past. Fear clutched her stomach. Noting the sensation, she took a step back.

Breathe, she told herself. *There's an answer to this. There's always an answer. We just have to find it.* Right now, she didn't know what that answer was. Danil was sick, but she would find a way to heal him. For now, they needed to find a way to safety.

"He needs rest," she said, words now calm. "There has to be somewhere safe we can go."

"We can't stop here." Marcus stood, face grim. "The noise will have the bigger packs headed this way. We need to leave, now."

As if to prove his point, a hollow war cry echoed through the valley. Marcus and Bastian lifted Danil onto Julianne's horse, where she cradled his lax body. Garrett, who had returned at hearing her cries for help, led her horse as Danil had just a day before.

The somber procession made their way back down the embankment and set off to continue their journey.

CHAPTER TWENTY-THREE

Danil roused twice during the day's travel, flailing his arms as though he was falling and once, lifting his head to look Julianne in the eyes.

"Danil?" she whispered, hope welling in her chest.

He bared his teeth, then sank back into unconsciousness.

"You dick bag," she muttered. "If you don't get through this, I'll never forgive you." She had to believe he would recover. If he didn't, she would never forgive herself.

They pressed on until late into the night, trying to put as much distance between them and the howling gang of remnant they'd heard earlier in the day. When they finally stumbled into a small clearing, the only preparation made was to designate a guard rotation, roll out sleeping mats, and collapse onto them.

Julianne laid Danil down with the help of the others, then settled in next to him. His breathing was steady and even, his eyes closed as if in a restful sleep. She hesitantly reached out to him with her mind. Before making contact, she withdrew.

Whatever was going on in his mind, she hadn't been able to push past it. He seemed peaceful and the quiet rest would probably help. Withdrawing, she let her eyes close against the flickering shadows beneath the bright moon.

A rough hand shook her awake, then pressed her mouth. Julianne's eyes shot open to see Bette leaning over her, shaking her head frantically. Julianne nodded and Bette carefully removed her hand.

What is it? She projected into the rearick's mind. Bette couldn't send an answer back, but it was clear in her thoughts. Garrett had woken her, and she'd immediately realized why. Though the sky had just begun to show streaks of vibrant pink and orange, the forest was silent. No birds, no chattering squirrels. A twig had snapped and Garrett had nodded knowingly.

Someone was nearby, and they were doing their best to hide it.

Julianne rose, careful not to disturb the leaves and sticks around her. Her eyes adjusted to the growing light quickly and she saw that she, Bette, Bastian, and Danil were alone. Marcus and Garrett were concealed in a tree, she quickly read in Bastian's mind.

They think it's a remnant party, Bastian sent. *They're not sure how many there are, and want to surprise them.* A quick image of Garrett and Marcus scaling nearby trees let Julianne know where they were.

No, don't look for them, she sent to Bastian, who'd reflexively tipped his head up. She reached down slowly to grasp her walking staff, hoping the movement would be hidden by the shadows. Bastian, she knew, was armed with a small magitech device, courtesy of Marcus. A brief memory of their last fight crossed her mind.

I've got this, Marcus showed me some moves while you slept last night. Bastian's mental projection was a confusing mix of fear, doubt, and resolute confidence.

She nodded grimly, eyes searching the forest for signs of movement. When it came, it was almost too late.

"Attack!" The shout went up as a handful of remnant burst into their camp simultaneously. Two went for Bastian, and one ran full tilt at Julianne.

She sprung to her feet, staff gripped across her body with both hands. A club slashed at her. The shock of the impact against her weapon vibrated through her arms.

"Die, whore!" the remnant screamed at her as a shadowed figure dropped from the sky behind it. Marcus shot the beast and its chest exploded, a cloud of flesh and stringy muscle erupting behind it.

"Behind you!" Julianne shouted.

Marcus spun just in time to parry a blow from another remnant. Metal clanged against metal again and again as Marcus tried to maneuver his weapon to get a blast in. Shouts from the other side of the camp drew her eyes to Bette in silent combat with another. The rearick was fast and precise, and she was *winning*.

Garrett, however, was not. Julianne sprinted over and swung her staff, the double-handed strike lashing out like a batting game that children played. Instead of a ball, her stick connected with spinal bones. The remnant collapsed, gurgling.

Help. Bastian's sharp, mental cry pierced Julianne's consciousness. She spun to find him across the camp in a defensive stance, waving his knife at two remnant while in his other hand, he frantically clicked the whirring magitech device. Danil lay at his feet, still and defenseless.

One of the remnant lunged forward at Bastian just as his weapon charged enough to send out a blast. The remnant twisted at the impact, but ignored the gush of blood as its shoulder disappeared, leaving one arm hanging limply by a few tendons.

They wrestled and, with Danil's defender otherwise occupied, the second remnant pounced on the unconscious mystic, arm raised to smash his head with a rock.

Time froze. Across the clearing, the rearick launched simultaneous blows as their opponents fell. Marcus had his weapon pointed, tip glowing as he prepared to fire on an enemy. All of them were too far away to help. Just like Julianne.

She reacted without thought, slamming her mind into Danil's attacker with every bit of force and focus she possessed. Sights and smells overwhelmed her as she plummeted through. Wolves gnashing teeth. Foxes rutting under moonlight. Fish gasping, dying as they drowned in the air.

Master! Bastian sent the strained cry soaked with the heady scent of bread, the taste of sweet elixir, and the feel of worn parchment. Images of stone walls and thick tapestries warred with the urge to bite, scratch, and mate.

The figure of Bethany Anne rose like a cross stitched goddess, the image from a hanging in the Temple entryway.

Julianne wrenched herself free of the dizzying images in the remnant's mind, doing as much damage as she could in the process. When her eyes cleared again, the figure over Danil wobbled. The rock dropped to one side, and the remnant collapsed only a moment before Bastian's knife plunged into its back.

Thank... Julianne's sending went unfinished as darkness closed over her for the second time since leaving the Temple.

CHAPTER TWENTY-FOUR

Marcus took the entire night shift on his own. He knew it was a stupid move—a twist of pain drove that thought home as he shifted and fresh blood seeped through the bandage Bette had bound his chest with earlier.

The fight ran through his mind over and over. As guilty as he felt for leaving Danil at risk, he knew that if he'd stayed close, Julianne or Bastian could just as easily have been hurt. The thought of Julianne falling into a stupor like Danil almost brought him to tears.

A twig snapped beside him and he spun, weapon ready.

"Settle down, lad," Bette admonished. "I just came out to see if you'd slept yet. By the shadows on yer face, I'm guessing not."

"I couldn't if I wanted to. Too jumpy from the fight." He forced a grin.

"Aye, that's a bullshit excuse if ever I heard one. You've got skills like a veteran, but yer still carrying the ego of a young one." Bette shook her head when Marcus tried to argue. "Don't bloody say ye don't. I can see it on yer face."

"It's not ego. I let two of our party members get hurt."

"You let them?" Bette raised a skeptical eyebrow. "Ye weren't hired on, lad, not by them. Yer only here as backup—*our* backup. If anything, it's me and Garrett that deserve a tongue lashing for letting the rest of ye down."

"But I've fought here, I know these monsters," Marcus hissed.

"Aye. And we know 'em, too. Oh, not like yerself, but enough to not let a bloody fiasco like that happen."

Marcus leaned back with a deep sigh, wincing as the breath caught in his pained side. "You're right. It's nobody's fault, and I'm an idiot for thinking it's mine."

She grinned broadly. "Now, give me a peek at those bandages. Ye need to thread it up, I'll bet." The grin fell away when she saw the soaked cloth. "Aye, lad. Ye need to get this seen to. How long until we hit the other side of this mess?"

Marcus grunted as Bette gently examined the area. "In our state, we'll be lucky to hit a village by nightfall. We'd be out of the hot zone now, if I hadn't been so worried about Danil."

Bette cursed. "Well, we can get to a safe place and clean it up, and I'll have a shot at stitching it meself, if yer willin'. I can't say I'm much of a seamstress, but I'll wager I'm better than Garrett."

"I heard that!" Garrett's muffled protest was soon joined by the man himself. "It's not polite, talkin' about a man's sewin' skills behind 'is back. Even if it *is* true."

"Out with ye, rearick. The lad don't be needin' any of yer sass." Bette shooed Garrett away. "Go and find him somethin' to eat. The poor wee thing's been up all night, look at the state of 'im!"

"Stubborn. All the young ones are," Garrett grumbled as he wandered off.

"You know I'm older than you, right?" Marcus called to his retreating back.

Once Bette had rebound his wound, Marcus went to sit by Julianne's side. He'd spent much of the night sitting on a fallen log, watching over her, willing her to wake up. When she'd collapsed, mumbling softly, his heart had almost burst.

"Come on, Jules. You're strong. You can get over this, I know you can."

"Marcus?" Julianne's dry mouth stifled the soft word. She worked her tongue, then tried again. "Marcus?"

"Julianne!" Soft hands cupped her head. "You're ok? Can you see?"

Julianne nodded. "I feel… ok, actually. What happened? My memory of last night is a bit spotty."

She tried to force her mind back to before she'd collapsed. The remnant, his mind feral and animalistic. Before that, her desperate bid to save— "Danil! Is he alive?" Fear clutched at her chest, making it difficult to breathe.

"He's fine, Jules. Hush." Marcus laid a hand on her, but she threw it off and sat up. "He hasn't woken yet, but you killed the remnant before it could lay a hand on Danil."

She squinted, her mind reaching for something forgotten. Then Julianne scrambled to her feet. "Bastian!" she called, loud and urgent.

Bastian shot up from his bedroll. "Yes, Master?"

Julianne strode towards Danil, still lying in the same spot she'd left him. A dark stain on the grass by his head fueled the excitement in her breast. "Bastian, you sent to me while I was attacking the remnant. Why did you send what you did?"

"I… I was watching your attack. I'm sorry, I know it was dangerous. I just wanted to see what it was like, in case you ended up like Danil. I thought maybe if that happened, if I saw it, I could help."

"Bastian, *why*. Why the bread, why the paper?"

Bastian blushed and dropped his eyes to the ground, uncertain. "It felt like you'd forgotten what it was like to be human. Like as soon as you entered that… that *thing's* head, you were one of them."

He paused, trying to remember what had spurred his automatic reaction. "When Mavis taught us about entering the mind of a person in a panic, she said that can happen. She told us it can make us panic, too, and the best way to ground yourself is to remember the present. I just... wanted you to remember, I guess."

Julianne paused. Then, maternal instinct took over, and she dashed over to envelop him in a tight hug. "You clever, clever boy."

Dropping him abruptly, she flew to Danil's side, crouched down and placed her hands on his head. The contact wasn't necessary, but would help her focus.

Danil.

She didn't enter his mind, instead cloaking herself in the feel of home. The musky smell of the Temple library. The gentle hum of the dining hall. Zoe, her bright face smiling in a shaft of sunlight. The leathery creases of Margit's hands. Cold, stone walls and footsteps so often trod that he didn't need to see to navigate.

Jules? Jules... I remember.

Tears slipped down Julianne's face as she bombarded him with memories, feelings, sensations from home.

Never thought I'd find you crying over me. Danil's wistful sending brought a joy like no other and she leaned down to wrap her arms around his limp body. When a shaking hand rose up to caress her hair, she sobbed.

Bitch and Bastard, Danil. I was so afraid.

You wouldn't bet against me, would you? Danil wriggled and she let go, helping him to sit. *You didn't even give me a chance to make any money off it.*

'How do you feel?" she asked, wiping her face.

"Like something the Bastard shat out after a hard night on the spirits." Danil scrunched his face and his eyes flickered white, then cleared. "Looks like I'm off the magic for a while, too. Damned if I wouldn't kill for a flask of elixir now. Or mead. Even that piss the rearick drink would do."

"Hey, now," Garrett said. "You lot are downright complimentary this morning, aren't ye?" He shook his head and continued over to the horses. "Glad yer back with us, Danil, but I'm afraid there's no rest fer the wicked. Yer soldier lad over there needs to make haste to the nearest town before he bleeds out like a gutted..." Garrett caught sight of Julianne's white face and immediately changed tack. "Er, well he needs some stitches is all. I'm sure the lad'll be fine."

Julianne bit her lip and Danil nudged her with one shoulder. "Go on. I'm not going anywhere. Except for a piss, so unless you want to help me with that?"

Julianne stood as Danil motioned Garrett over for some assistance. She headed to Marcus, who sat talking with Bette. His eyes didn't leave Julianne's face, despite the serious conversation they seemed to be having.

"Marcus, you didn't tell me you were hurt!"

"That's because he's a man. Stubborn, they are," Bette proclaimed. "He'll live as long as it heals over and stays clean, though he'll have a scar to show for it."

"Do we have anything to clean out wounds?" Julianne asked, frowning. One of the stipulations of the rearick contracts stated that they were responsible for bringing equipment for emergencies.

"Aye, but it needs a proper goin' over, and I don't think making him bleed all over the hot zone is the best idea."

"How far?" Julianne asked, repeating Bette's earlier question.

"A half day's walk should get us somewhere safe enough." Julianne frowned, and Marcus explained. "There's a good chance the remnant who attacked us were from the same area as the one that fell and died. They were likely in her pack, and followed us. It's unusual to find a group hunting this close to the Madlands edge."

"Marcus, how could you know that? You said yourself, you've never been this side."

"The intelligence comes through regularly. More traders are

crossing the borders and keeping us updated. Look, it's no guarantee, but I'm confident." *And I don't want to ride all bloody day with a hole in my side.*

Julianne nodded, as much at his words as the trail of thought that followed them. "I trust you." She meant it. This man was their leader, and she would follow him to the ends of the world.

Marcus quirked a smile. "Thank you. That means a lot."

"As much as I hate to break up this little chat, we really should be goin'," Garrett said. "Bastian's packed the gear, and Danil said he feels ok to travel, so if yer all well enough to make a move?"

Marcus nodded. "Thanks, Garrett. And you, too, Bette. You've done a hell of a job patching me up."

CHAPTER TWENTY-FIVE

They moved out slowly, Julianne turning her head away from the bodies piled up by the side of the trail.

Garrett said that'll scare off any other packs that come this way, Bastian sent as they passed it.

Anything that helps, I guess. She paused, then launched into something she'd been stewing on all morning. *Bastian, I'm sorry. I shouldn't have attacked the remnant like I did, not after what happened to Danil.*

You don't need to apologize to me. You're my leader, not the other way around. I'm just glad you're ok. Bastian ducked under a low branch, then glanced back to make sure Julianne did the same.

Being a leader doesn't mean doing what you want. It's a responsibility. It's my job to make sure you and Danil, and everyone back at the Temple and even the pilgrims are as safe as I can make them. What I did yesterday went against that. If you hadn't pulled me back, you'd be stuck out here alone with two catatonic mystics to take care of.

Julianne rubbed her head absentmindedly. It still ached, but it was due to overwork now. The bruise behind her ear was almost gone and only tender to touch.

But because you did, Danil's ok. This sending came with a flood of emotion, both tender and grateful.

Thank you, Bastian, but I think you had more to do with that than I did.

The boy prickled with embarrassed pride, but didn't reply. Julianne slipped back into her own thoughts, while quietly keeping tabs on Bette, who rode with Danil, and Marcus, who shifted more and more uncomfortably as the morning progressed.

Eventually, Julianne pushed her horse up ahead to join him. "If you stop for a little, I can ease the pain for you."

"I can't," Marcus grunted. The morning warmth didn't warrant the sweat beading on his head. "If I can't feel it, I'm more likely to do it more harm."

"I can prevent that," she said. "I can take away the tedious pain, the constant, wearing hurt. I'll leave the sharp pain, the signal pain alone."

"You can do that?" he asked, surprised.

She winked. "I can do a lot of things to a man's body without him even knowing."

Marcus gaped. Then he shook himself and lifted a hand to call a halt. "Do I need to dismount?"

"No," Julianne said. "But for deep work, it helps to touch. Give me your hands."

He took one of her hands gently, then the other, like lovers in a handfasting ceremony. Julianne quickly banished the errant thought and mumbled a word to help her begin. She touched his pain, followed each tendril and read the messages it took. Some she numbed, others she left.

"How does that feel?" she asked, still holding his hand.

"It feels good. Really… ow!" He flexed his body, yelping as his pain sensors admonished him for it.

"Working as intended, then." The rough warmth of Marcus's hand brushed her senses. Out of nowhere, a hot tide of desire washed over her, and she dropped it quickly.

"Thanks. Ready to go?"

Julianne took a breath to clear her head. "Just give me a minute." Julianne slipped into a deeper trance with some difficulty. Her usually stable emotions seemed shot, and for some reason, she couldn't shake the sudden need that drowned her when she looked at Marcus.

Oh, for goodness sake, she snapped at herself. Julianne clenched her muscles then relaxed them and reached out with her mind. She pushed past the discomfort and fatigue, stretching as far as she could. Just as she was about to give up, she felt it. A flicker of consciousness on the outskirts of her range.

"We need to go that way." She lifted an arm to point, gripping the saddle to keep steady. She hadn't entirely recuperated from last night, and working on Marcus had sapped more of her mental energy.

"Are you ok?" Marcus caught her as she swayed.

"Yeah, I'm just… starving?" She'd eaten that morning and shouldn't be this *hungry*. Shaking, she rummaged in her bags and pulled out a cloth bag. She crammed a handful of jerky in her mouth, blushing in embarrassment.

"So, what's that way?" Marcus asked.

"People." The word came out garbled around a mouthful of food. Julianne forced it down and tried again. "I can sense people, or at least a person. It can't be too far, or I wouldn't be able to. Not in the state I'm in."

Marcus cocked an eyebrow. "And what state is that?"

Still reeling from the sudden bursts of heat and hunger, Julianne clamped down on her mind. He couldn't use magic to see her thoughts, but right now, she couldn't trust a damn thing about herself.

"I'm just tired." She slowed her horse and moved to one side, waiting until Danil passed before moving in beside him.

"Hey, Jules," he said before she spoke.

"I thought you were too worn out for magic?" she teased.

"I am. I can sense *you* from a mile away, but that has nothing to do with magic." He smiled, turning his face not quite in her direction. His green eyes were pale in the bright daylight.

"Danil… how are you feeling? Since you woke up, I mean."

He shrugged. "It's taken a toll on me, for sure. A day without food has given me a beast of an appetite, and a temper to match."

"You? A temper?" Julianne laughed. Danil was a rascal, with his sharp wit and a taste for gaming, but she'd never seen him in a foul mood before.

"I know." His face looked like a whipped puppy. "I snapped at Garrett for trying to help with my breakfast, then ran poor Bastian off just for asking how I felt one too many times. Truth be told, it was only the second time he'd asked."

Julianne winced. "I've been feeling a bit… unusual, myself." She didn't elaborate and when she glanced over at Danil, he'd sunk into his own thoughts.

Julianne? Bastian caught her attention and again, she shuffled her place in the line.

"What is it?" she asked. The base of her skull was now throbbing in time to the slow beat of hooves, and the sun was just a little too hot.

"I wondered how you were feeling." Bastian spoke carefully, as if unsure how his words would be received.

"Bastian, it's ok. Danil is a bit of a bear this morning. I think he's just tired."

"That's just it, though." Bastian's eyes glinted as if he'd found cake. "You see, I've been probing his mind since he woke, yours as well, and there's something there, Master Julianne. A residue or a feeling, I can't quite describe it but it's almost exactly like—"

She cut off his excited torrent of words. "You were probing my mind? Today?"

"Um. Yes? I'm sorry, I know the rules outside the Temple are different, I didn't mean to cause offense." Bastian's face turned a deep shade of purple as he tried to backtrack his words.

"No." Julianne waved away his concerns. "I'm not angry, just annoyed at myself for not noticing."

"That's just it, though!" Bastian said. "Julianne, what I can feel in your minds is the same feeling I had when I was on your coat-tails earlier. When you went into Danil's head, while the memory of the beast-woman still had him and when the same thing was trying to draw you in, *that's still there inside you.*"

Panic rose in her chest and she snapped, "Don't be stupid. You can't catch something using mental magic. You're imagining it." She bared her teeth at him, heart pounding.

"See?" he crowed. "You're doing it now! Reacting like your animal urge is taking over."

Her hand gripped her walking staff, still tied to the saddle. Her knuckles were white with the effort.

"Everything ok up there?" Garrett called from behind.

Julianne looked down at her hand, still on the staff.

"Bastian, I…"

She what? Had been about to attack him for sharing a theory? For frightening her with the idea it may have been right?

Cocking her head to one side, she realized Bastian was inside it, soothing her panic. He flinched when she noticed him, but she simply watched as he worked. The boy had a sharp mind, that was for sure, and seemed to have an affinity for the emotions.

Within moments, she was able to slip into a contemplative meditation. She didn't use magic, instead turning his words over in her head, trying to make sense of them. What she'd said was true—magic was simply a projection of thought. You couldn't catch a disease, or keep a part of someone's mind with you.

And yet, she realized there was a precedent for this. Any mystic who'd worked on a person with mental illness—or after severe trauma—knew it could manifest in the days after. It wasn't an effect of the magic, not directly.

However, slipping into a memory of someone watching her husband die a sudden, painful death was just as real to the mystic as it was to the patient. Even though the deceased may be a stranger, for the duration of the spell, it *was* their husband. Even after disconnecting it could feel like the mystic had just lost a loved one.

"So, you think it's a stress-based reaction?" Bastian had been reading her thoughts again.

"Perhaps. But, now that I'm aware of it, I think there may be more to it."

Bastian frowned, not understanding. "Like, a kind of trans-ference?"

"No. Bastian, when you go back to the Temple, do you think things will be different? Will it feel the same, or will it be smaller, plainer now that you've seen the world?"

"Well," he began, then paused to chew on the question. "I suppose it won't be the same. I don't feel as chafed out here, as stifled. I hadn't realized I felt that way back home, but now that I've really been outside… But I don't understand how that relates to the remnant, though."

Julianne worried at her lip, wondering how to explain. She wanted words for this, as they would have to be recorded later, for research purposes. "The remnant are animals, in the most basic sense of the word. Oh, they're intelligent enough. Clearly, they can speak and plan, they just lack… something. Inhibitions, fear, common sense?"

She fell silent for a moment, thinking. "They don't have any responsibility. I, on the other hand, have grown up with it. First while running my parents' house for them, then as a favored student, now as Master. Expectations, every day. Oh, I don't mind them, but I've often wondered what life is like for someone who has nothing to do with their day but keep a house and milk some cows."

"And… you got a taste of that?" Bastian said. His eyes were

narrowed, as if trying to glean any extra bit of information he could gather.

"More than a taste." Julianne smiled softly, remembering the sensation of wind over a mountaintop. "I imagine it's similar to what a druid would feel, inhabiting the mind of a bird in flight."

Then, the memory of the sensations that started all this came to mind and she kicked her horse forwards, shuttering her mind in case the young mystic tried to read it again.

"Thank you for talking to me, Bastian," she called over her shoulder.

CHAPTER TWENTY-SIX

The tiny cottage looked out of place amongst the tall grasses and broken fence. Whitewashed walls gleamed in the afternoon sun and bright flowers lined the windows, beckoning to the tired travelers like honey to a bee.

They had pushed hard in the early hours, slowing as the terrain thinned and all signs of the cloistered jungle the remnant called home faded.

Marcus had tried to keep on, but Bette forced a stop for lunch when he swayed in his sleep. The soldier had a seemingly endless amount of fortitude, though. After some food and a fifteen-minute nap, he climbed astride again and insisted he was fit to go.

Still, Bette thought, he was only human. Marcus sweated and his normally brown face was white and sickly. How he found the energy to kick his horse into a trot when the tiny farm came into view, she'd never know.

They approached carefully. All Julianne had been able to tell them is which direction to head. The girl didn't have much more color than Marcus, and by the way she rubbed her head, a thumping headache, too.

Bette slid off her horse and handed the reins to Garrett. "I'll knock," she said. "So that *yer* ugly face doesn't get the door slammed in it. Ye'll take care of the others?"

He nodded seriously, and she trusted he understood what she had meant: she would approach the farm, as the less threatening of the two, and he would stay back to protect their charges if anything went wrong.

The little brass knocker was tarnished but smooth. Bette rapped on the door three times, then reeled back as a barrage of angry barks startled her.

"Who's there?" The voice that called out was rasped, but had a strong edge to it.

"Travelers," Bette called back, trying to sound friendly. "We seek refuge after days of hard travel through the Madlands." She didn't want to admit they had injured people, not yet.

The door opened a small crack, a glittering chain stretched behind it to stop it opening further. A wrinkled face squinted out, eyes dropping to Bette. "Oh. You're not with them priests, are you? I won't have none of that foolery inside my house." Lower down, a black snout pressed against the opening and growled, teeth bared.

"Priests? No. We're just travelers," Bette answered.

"From?"

"Arcadia." It was close enough, and Bette guessed most outsiders wouldn't have heard of the Heights. "We came across the Madlands."

The door slammed, then opened properly this time. "Mind your manners, Florence. These are guests. Until I say otherwise at least. Hear me?"

Apparently, Florence was the dog. She dropped her hackles and sat, watching the visitors warily, but content with her mistress's instructions for now.

"We apologize for the intrusion," Bette said. "But we wondered if ye have room fer us to sleep? We've injured with us, and just need a day of shelter so we can recover. The barn would be fine." She had spotted the old building behind the house. It looked weatherproof, if not much more.

"I'll be having none of that rubbish. You'll stay inside, where I can keep an eye on you. I'll feed you dinner, breakfast, too. The cost is a couple of beds weeded and some shingles on the roof fixed. If you're needing a second night, there's a field to be tilled. By hand, mind. Got no horses left and the donkey died last month."

Bette nodded. She knew how to hand-till a field and damned if Garrett wouldn't be helping. "We'd be happy to help."

The old woman hobbled inside, her gait as crooked as the hump on her back. "The pale one, is he sick or wounded? I'd be guessing the latter, seeing as where you've been and all."

"Wounded," Bette admitted. She quickly eyed the house. Only one water glass on the table, and two of the three dining chairs were covered in dust. The old woman lived alone. Bette motioned the others in. "Is there somewhere we can put our horses?"

"In the barn. Rub them down, and let them graze in the field out back. The Goddess knows there's enough there for them to eat, and it could do with some thinning out.

Bette thanked her and headed out, catching Bastian's arm on his way in. "I'll need some help with the horses."

"Of course," he said.

They took the horses from Garrett and led them into the barn. It was a wide, airy space that sent clouds of dust as the floor was disturbed.

Bette showed Bastian how to lay out their tack and brush the horses down, a task she and Garrett had taken care of while travelling. A burr on a horse's back could cause a pile of grief under a saddle, and their mornings on the trail were rushed and disorganized. Here, she would have time to check them over before they rode out again.

"Did ye get a peek in the old woman's head?" she asked as they worked.

"Yes," Bastian said. "Only a quick one. She has some rudimentary shielding ability, but nothing as strong as a trained magician."

"I assume she's safe, then, or ye wouldn't be out here." Bette slapped her horse's back side, sending it out to munch on the long grass outside before moving to brush down Cloud Dancer.

"I think so. She seems wary, like there's trouble she's not telling us about. She trusts us for some reason, though."

"And ye think she's got some kind of magic?" Bette raised her eyebrows, skeptical.

"I wouldn't go that far," Bastian said. "Probably just used to the occasional traveler. Marcus said that's pretty much the only way through the Madlands without adding another three days to the journey."

"Aye, I suppose." Finished with the second horse, Bette wandered outside.

She soon spotted the water pump, and an old trough that was still in decent enough shape to hold water. Bucketing water into the trough, she explained the basics of horse care to Bastian. "The water is warm, so the horses can drink. If ye ever feed a horse cold water after a ride like that, it'll likely be dead by morning."

They finished up and Bette insisted they wash before going in, then chastised Bastian for attempting to step inside with his muddy boots still on.

"This woman has let us into her house, don't you *dare* go slopping mud on her floor. And if anyone leaves so much as a plate unwashed, the Bitch will smite ye down and bless ye with an ugly wife, if I don't get to ye first."

"Thank you, young lady. It's good to see some manners in these parts again. They've all but gone by the wayside in recent days." The old woman wiped her hands on her apron and shook Bette's hand.

Bette stole a look around at the room. The old farmhouse had been grand once and was still well looked after, but age had taken its toll.

"I'm Mariana, but you can call me Annie. Most do. Most don't deserve to, but that's another matter. I sent your friends out to wash. Have you eaten a midday meal?"

Bastian ducked his head self-consciously. "Yes, thank you. We really don't mean to impose, we can leave some of our supplies behind—"

"Oh, don't you worry about that. Since my boys left, the garden's been serving up more than I can eat. Can you peel potatoes?"

"Yes, ma'am. In the Temple, I was—"

"Temple?" Annie interrupted him again. "I thought you said you weren't no priests." She narrowed her eyes at Bette.

"Not priests. Mystics. They have the power of the mind?" She'd heard stories about odd beliefs in the villages across the Madlands, but this woman didn't even know what a mystic was?

Annie frowned, then let out a sigh. "Well, you don't talk like them at least. You asked instead of told me you'd be staying. Least you're not wearing them ridiculous robes. Oh, no offence to you, young man, at least yours are somewhat humble. No, the priests around here like gold in their thread and silk in their britches." Old timbers creaked as voices filtered through the hallway. "Looks like your friends have finished unpacking."

Marcus and Julianne came in and Bette shot them a questioning look.

"Danil is going to lie down for a little," she explained. "And Garrett went off to scout the area."

Bette nodded and looked to Annie. "Is there somewhere I can stitch up my friend? The wound isn't too bad, but it'll at least need cleaning again. I dinna want to poke at it on the road with all those beasts about."

"I could do without it being poked at entirely, thanks." Marcus twisted his mouth into a tired smile.

"You just sit him at the table here, and I'll go put some water on to boil." Annie moved towards the back room, but paused at the door. "Do you have needle and thread?"

"Aye," Bette said. "I just need good light and a wee bit of water."

Annie sent Bastian outside to gather some vegetables for their dinner, her instructions echoing loudly from the kitchen. "You do know what beans are, don't you? Never can tell what they've got in these foreign lands."

He scurried off with firm instructions not to come back until his bowl was full.

Marcus stretched back in the wooden chair and closed his eyes. "If I flinch, it's because I'm tired, right? Not because I'm in pain, or terrified of a tiny little needle like that." He studied the tool as Bette expertly threaded the eye.

"What? Big brute like you, fighting out there, and you're scared of a wee needle?"

Rather than argue, Marcus just grit his teeth. He didn't notice when Julianne quietly slipped in, Annie on her heels.

CHAPTER TWENTY-SEVEN

"So, Annie," Bette said as she cleaned the wound. "It sounds like ye been having some trouble in these parts. Some people in fancy robes?" She shot a look at Julianne, who stayed silent but leaned in to listen.

The mystic's eyes, however, were on Marcus's stretched, muscular torso. Bette wondered if her tongue was about to fall on the ground. She shook her head, then carefully pierced Marcus with the needle. He tensed and sucked in a sharp breath.

"Yes, that's right. Moved in a few months ago, they did. A whole tribe of them, and their prissed up leader in his jewels and finery."

"What did their robes look like?" Julianne asked.

At her voice, Marcus's eyes shot open. With a weak smile, he glanced once at the strand of thread pulled out from his side, and closed them again, suddenly still and quiet.

"Blue, with golden trims and pretty gems on their buttons. Funny little sun shape on the sleeves, I guess because of the name they gave themselves."

"The New Dawn," Julianne said softly.

Annie looked surprised. "Yes, that's them. I take it you've had dealings with them before?"

"You could say that." Julianne's voice was carefully neutral, but Annie wasn't fooled.

"They take someone of yours, too?"

"Take them? They killed two of the Temple Guards. They were my friends," she added, face hard. "If their words are true, they mean to do much worse than that."

"You mean like take a village hostage with their mind tricks, leaving children to starve while their parents work to the bone? Taking men from their homes and setting them to work the farms and the mills, for no pay and no food and discarding them when they work themselves to an injury?"

"Bitch take me," Julianne muttered, her eyes widening a bit.

"There'll be no use of the Goddess's name like that in my house, I'll thank you." Annie tapped her left breast with two fingers.

"Of course. I'm sorry, Annie. Where we come from, the Bitch and the Bastard are... worshipped quite differently." Julianne spoke carefully, not wanting to offend the woman who'd taken them in.

"Fair enough. I heard about some strange religions over the border, so I don't blame you for having your ways." Annie ducked her head. "Though if you've got the magic, that no doubt changes things anyway. You're touched by the Goddess?"

"Touched?" Julianne asked. "You mean with magic?" Annie nodded. "Ahh. The teachings in our land say that everyone has the capacity for magic. Some are just stronger than others. I'm... well, quite strong, but only in mental magic."

"Many of our preachers say the same, that the Goddess has touched all, but some got a helping heap of her favor. They're the ones what can do the real magic. Not like me, all I can do is whistle the plants up and keep them growing. Not that I need that now." Annie cast a forlorn look at the mantelpiece. On it were two hats, both overly large for the frail old woman.

"Annie, who did the New Dawn take from you?" Julianne asked quietly.

"My sons." Annie coughed, clearing the sudden huskiness in her voice. "They resisted, better than most. Eventually, they fell to the magic of the priests. That's no act of the Goddess. What those assholes do? Remnant have more heart." Her eyes glittered and Julianne reluctantly dropped her probing questions.

Instead, she dropped her eyes and fiddled with her dress, trying to calm her mind enough to ignore the nagging headache. It was no good. The smell of coppery blood soaked the air, sending a frisson of anxiety along her skin. Her thoughts jangled inside her head, unwilling to sit still or give her the space to block them out.

Julianne wanted to pace, to work off the nervous energy. She wanted to growl and curse and rip the heads off the people perverting her magic. She wanted to avenge Annie, a woman she barely knew but cared about the moment she'd invited them in. Most of all, she wanted to grab Marcus's pretty face and press her...

Shoving her chair back with a screech, Julianne quickly stepped over to the nearest window, pretending to look out. She rested her head against the cool glass and willed the flames from her cheeks.

And with Marcus? What in the ever-loving world am I thinking? She thought. *Bitches oath, but I'll be glad when this wears off.* At least she had the sense to lock down her shields.

Vaguely, she realized the conversation had turned from religion. Raging emotions now tightly under control, Julianne turned back.

Annie peeked over at Marcus. "That wound doesn't look good."

"No," Bette said as she tied off the stitching. "I have some antiseptic, though. It should be enough to fix it."

"That some kind of standard issue stuff? My husband, bless his soul, did a term with the rangers up in Arsa. The stuff they hand out is weaker than a crooked barman's beer."

Bette shrugged wryly. "Seems some things are the same wherever ye go."

Annie stood. "I've some tincture of lavender and seal. It'll sting, but it'll clear that fester up in no time."

"I might check on Bastian," Julianne said.

She followed Annie to the kitchen and through the back, almost bumping into Garrett as he returned.

"Everything well?" she asked in a low voice.

"Aye," he said. "No sign of remnant this far out, and the nearest farmhouse was abandoned."

That gave Julianne a measure of unease, but she waved him in the direction of the dining room and left him to it.

The vegetable garden, a small, fenced-off section of the overgrown farm, looked like an absolute jungle. Tomatoes stretched high, stalks strong despite the lack of trellises for support. A pumpkin vine wound its way over one fence, and a thick, bushy plant dripping with beans over another. Seeing the untouched beans, Julianne frowned. Bastian should be almost done by now, and she expected more from him than to shirk off such a simple duty.

The gate screeched in protest as she pushed it open and a dark head popped up from the back corner. "Master Julianne! I'm sorry, am I taking too long?" Dirt smudged Bastian's face, and a leaf jutted from his hair.

"What in the world are you doing?" Julianne carefully picked her way through a matted clump of thyme surrounding an overloaded eggplant, then took a large step to straddle an overgrown parsley. "Aren't you supposed to be getting beans?"

Bastian held up a wooden bowl. "I did! Julianne, this garden…

the old lady must have some kind of druid magic. These plants are as healthy as I've ever seen. The weeds are atrocious, though."

Julianne finally got close enough to see what he'd been doing. A pile of scraggly, uprooted weeds lay in the corner, while a large square patch of garden had been freshly tidied. The soft brown dirt had been smoothed over, and a drooping vine wound back over the fence posts.

"Wow." Julianne looked at him with new admiration. "You've really made a difference here."

"It needs a lot more work. If you don't mind, I'd like to keep going. After the trip we've had, it feels good to sink my hands into something familiar." Bastian waggled his dirty fingers.

"Actually, that's why I came out. My brain is still too fried to mind-read, and I really need to know what the New Dawn have been up to here. I wondered if you could look at Annie's memories to see what's been going on."

"Ah." A crestfallen look crossed Bastian's face, making Julianne hesitate.

"It can wait," she said. "Here, I'll take the beans in. Just make sure you wash up before you come inside."

"What is it with women?" Bastian grumbled, just loud enough for Julianne to hear. "It's not like I was born in a barn."

She hid a smile and hoisted the bowl to her shoulder and carried it inside.

"Annie?" she called, depositing it on the counter. "I've got the beans, Bastian wants to continue working in the garden."

"Working?" Annie ducked into the kitchen, face glowing. "I must say it's appreciated. My back isn't what it was and now my boys aren't here to help, I just haven't been keeping up with things like I should be."

Julianne chewed her lip. "Annie, how would you feel about putting us up for a few more days? I can pay in Arcadian coin, and we'll do what we can to help while we're here. Between us, we should be able to make some progress."

"Well now, that would be just wonderful. My big old house has been far too quiet, I was already beginning to think I'd miss you when you're all gone." She smiled at Julianne, the wrinkles in her face creasing around it. "Keep your coin. If you're happy to work for your keep, that'll do me just fine."

CHAPTER TWENTY-EIGHT

Bastian didn't come in until dinner time, by which time Garrett had been roped into helping him fix the fallen fence around the garden. Bette re-shingled the roof of the chicken coop while Marcus watched on, and Julianne mucked out the long-abandoned horse stalls. When dusk fell and the temperature dropped, they tumbled inside with dirt on their clothes and smiles on their faces.

"Go on, straight to the basin with you. You're not going to traipse that mud through my house, not over my dead body." Despite Annie's admonishments, Julianne could feel the relief emanating from her bones.

Instead of worrying about rats breeding in the stables or her chickens freezing in the winter, she'd gained a slight reprieve from the work that had been piling up. The vegetable garden was now weed-free and properly fenced off from roaming pigs, and had yielded a bounty of food carefully prepared for the evening meal.

"Annie, lass, this is the best feed I've had in a long time," Garrett gushed through a mouthful of potato. He piled mushrooms on top of his fork and shoved another lump in his mouth.

"Yes, I suppose it would be," Annie said. "On account of you being on the road and all."

"Oh, it's been years since I've eaten this well." He licked a clump of beet sauce off his whiskers.

"Annie, really, it's a beautiful meal," Julianne said. Looking down at her plate she added, "Do you often cook for a horde like ours?"

Annie scowled. "If you have a question, girl, ask it."

Julianne mentally gave the woman a point. "What happened to your sons? And the town—you said the New Dawn had been taking people. Can you tell us more?"

Glaring down at her plate, Annie stabbed a limp bean and held it up for scrutiny. "They came a few months ago, touting their status as Goddess-touched. Seemed like a fair claim, they certainly had magic—but no Goddess of mine would have sanctioned what they did with it."

"And what was that?" Bastian asked.

"Used it like that opium syrup what ravaged Arsa a few decades back. They'd ask a small favor and when it was done, their eyes would glow white and the person they were talking to would fall back, like in a rapture. If the favor was declined, they'd instead walk away with a terrible itch on the mind. Not a real one, just a certainty that something wasn't right, that they'd just done something terrible. Been on the end of that one more than once," she admitted.

"They all had the same magic?" Julianne asked.

"A little." Annie shrugged. She'd pushed her plate away a little as if she'd lost her appetite. "But mostly it was August, their leader. He was the one who was most gifted in that way."

Julianne stifled a curse. August wasn't who she'd come to find. Still, he might know where Rogan was, if she could get to him. Either way, what he'd done to the village couldn't continue.

Bette tapped her fork on the plate. "So, the Dawn was using

pleasure to make the villagers addicted to them? Sounds like something out of a children's tale."

"Ain't no difference to me if you believe it," Annie said.

"Oh, I wasn't saying I didn't. Just that it'd take a real twat to come up with something like that. Err, sorry, Annie." Bette winced as she remembered Annie's thoughts on cursing.

"Can't argue with you there. Real twats. Yup, that's about the sum of them." She passed Bette a wink, which drew a crooked smile in response.

"You can't be telling me they can control a whole town like that, can you?" Marcus sat upright, carefully still to avoid aggravating his wound. Somehow, he still looked ready to leap into battle and strike down the villains who'd taken Annie's sons.

Annie hefted a sigh. "Sounds crazy, I know. But once a person gets to liking the rewards, that's it. Those who tended to the drink and the smoke went first, and a few of the mothers who enjoyed a particular herb tea a little too much. Old Weyland was an early convert, after they fixed his joints."

"Fixed them how?" Bastian asked.

"Well, he says they don't hurt no more. They're still as lumpy and chapped as ever, but he does say he can't feel the pain no more."

"Mind trick," Bastian muttered.

Annie darted her eyes up. "You mean he's not healed? He just thinks he can't feel it?"

Bastian nodded, and Annie collapsed in on herself, just the smallest bit.

"Why, Annie?" Julianne prodded gently.

"Max, my son. He has a wife, a pretty thing if she ain't too bright. Susie… well, she had a lump in the back of her throat. We all know how those things tend to end up. Wouldn't get it cut out, said she'd never, even if we dragged her to a surgeon kicking and screaming." Annie shook her head, mouth tight. "Anyway, not too long ago, Susie came running home, said those Dawn folk had fixed it. She couldn't feel the lump no more, and the pain she'd had was gone. She opened her mouth to show and… well, I thought it was just my old eyes couldn't see any different."

"That's when your wee Max joined them?" Bette twisted her mouth as if she'd bitten into something sour. "All for a bloody trick. Annie, no matter what these people say, there's no such thing as healing magic."

"Well that's a bloody lie," Garrett exclaimed. "Hannah can heal! And them druids, too. What, ye didn't hear the stories?"

Annie perked up at his words, but Julianne raised a hand to ward off his claims. "Hannah is a special case. The druids can heal, yes, but they can't play with minds like a mystic."

"I don't know this Hannah girl, or what a druid is, but I'm reading your words to say there ain't much chance our Susie is really better."

Julianne nodded, her face grave.

"It's alright." Annie speared another vegetable, looked at it, then put it back on her plate and pushed it away. "I thought as much when it happened. Bess always had an eye for that kind of thing." Annie calmly took a swallow of water.

"Bess?" Julianne asked.

"My cat. She took a fancy to Susie, but when she got sick, that cat was the first to know. Went and sat on her lap and never left her side after, even when she said she'd been cured." Annie abruptly stood and began to clear the table.

Garrett and Bette jumped up to help, snatching plates away from each other in an effort to carry the most. Julianne stretched and yawned. "Bette," she called. "I made a plate for Danil. Could you pop it in the cold room so it's there for him later?"

"No, don't." Julianne swung around to see Danil behind her, his eyes white as he walked confidently into the room.

"Danil! I didn't know you'd woken." Julianne felt her muscles sag with relief at seeing his magic had returned.

"Just in time for you to go to bed," he replied.

"No, I'm fine—"

"Don't be a fool, Jules." Danil grinned to soften the sting of his words. "Everyone in this room is trying to think of a way to tell you how awful you look. Go on; you get to bed. I won't let you sleep too late, I've already missed too much."

Julianne stopped on her way past to wrap her arms around him. "I'm glad you're ok," she murmured.

"Except for the pit in my stomach." He laughed as it let out a growl. "Where's that food?"

Julianne left Danil to the care of the others and traipsed upstairs to bed. The bags were in the doorway of the larger room where she'd left them, and the fresh sheets smelled of lavender.

She untied her set laces, then gave up and collapsed onto the mattress fully dressed. By the time she'd dragged the blankets over her shoulders, she was fast asleep.

CHAPTER TWENTY-NINE

When she cracked an eye open the next morning to find sunlight streaming through the window, Julianne was surprised to find her mind loose and relaxed. The days of riding, coupled with the stress of the mission and later, her run in with the remnant, had left her with a near permanent headache and a band of tightness that ran from the base of her skull down her back.

She stretched and sighed peacefully, unwilling to leave the warm blankets. Noises downstairs suggested everyone was up, so eventually Julianne rolled out of bed and stripped off her wrinkled clothes and dressed in clean ones. Bette's bag had been moved and lay open, but Julianne had slept so soundly, she'd never noticed the rearick come to the bed they'd agreed to share.

She stepped out into the upstairs hall and almost ran into Garrett, who was carrying a folded set of sheets into the room the men had shared.

"Oh look, it's sleeping beauty." He grinned and she swatted him.

"Why didn't someone wake me?" she asked.

"Danil's fault, not mine. Though he did try to lay a wager that at least one person would feel the back of yer hand for it."

"I hope you didn't bet against him then," she shot back.

"Do I look like a fool?" He peeked at her over the pile of linen, his short beard pressing down on top of it to keep it from toppling. Julianne didn't answer, just raised an eyebrow. "Aye, well, blame me mam for that. And a night on the couch. Your Danil might have to take it tomorrow night if he doesn't reign in that cheek of his."

"He's not *my* Danil," Julianne retorted and rolled her eyes at the rearick. Downstairs, the table had already been laid with plates of bacon, beans and bread, and a big jar of honey was being passed around.

"Good morning. Annie, I'm sorry I overslept."

"It's of no matter to me; I'm not your keeper. The chores have been done for the day, and I appreciate the help of your friends. I suppose you're going into town later?"

Marcus choked on his bread. "You mean towards the psychotic cult that brainwashes everyone in their path? I don't think so."

Annie raised an eyebrow. "Ain't nobody ask questions like you all did yesterday unless you're planning to go into the jaws of the mountain cat."

Julianne cut off Marcus's protest. "That's exactly what I intend to do," she said. "Will you help us? With information, I mean."

Annie nodded. "Seems like if anyone's going to sort this mess out, it'd best be done sooner than later. That's the last of the bacon I stored over winter, and I don't like being without."

"Jules," Danil said, hurriedly swallowing a large mouthful of bread. "There's something else. I was talking to Annie late last night, and it seems Artemis has passed through here."

Julianne almost choked. "Really? You saw him?"

"Yes." Annie dabbed her mouth with a napkin. "Crazy as he was, he seemed to have a good heart. Well, most of one anyway. Not real useful around a farm, though."

"Do you know where he went?" Julianne held her breath. If he was near, was it worth risking a trip into the town?

Annie regarded her shrewdly. "What's your plan?"

Julianne turned to look at the old woman in the eye. "To destroy the New Dawn. If they've really taken people as slaves, they need to be held accountable. I will bring that reckoning if no one else can, or will." She waited for the words to sink in before continuing. "I don't know if I can do it alone, though. My strength relies on mind magic, and the New Dawn have found a way to block it somehow. I think—I *hope*—Artemis knows how to defeat them."

"And why would he know that?" Annie's voice held an edge to it. Julianne debated lying to the woman, but knew her conscience wouldn't allow it.

"Because I think he taught them to do it." Annie slumped as if knowing the words were coming. "Annie, I don't know Artemis, but I know people who do. They all tell me he's a good person, that he wouldn't hurt a fly. They also said he can be easily distracted, and that he didn't really understand people."

Annie nodded. "Sounds about right. I never suspected the man of doing us wrong on purpose, but he's a few loaves short of a bread basket, that one. He and little Lilly are the same. Odd, but still good people." Annie's face creased with sadness. "I hope he took the girl with him. Goddess knows she'd be safer off in the hills."

With some prodding, Annie explained that Lilly was one of the village children. She was touched by the Goddess and had the skill to talk to animals and trees, but it had apparently addled her brain.

"They apprenticed her to me for a time, on account of my talent with the growing things," she explained. "Girl was beyond me, though. Where I can tend a garden and make it flourish, Lilly had the gift of beast talking. Even the mountain cats would cuddle her like a doll, and the birds and squirrels followed her like a lady's handmaidens."

A druid? Danil sent to Julianne.

Perhaps. They both show signs of it, but neither have had teaching, so they won't have all the skills. Ezekiel would be able to shed more light on it. Julianne sent the reply by reflex, then jolted upright, realizing what it meant.

"What is it, Jules?" Marcus asked from the other end of the table.

"Nothing. I just hadn't noticed my magic was back." She smiled self-consciously, wondering if her reaction had been that obvious, or if he'd been watching her.

"I think it makes sense to try find the old man first," Marcus said, looking to Garrett for support.

"And if we canna find him, or he canna help?" the rearick asked. "Or if we scout the town, and realize the help he gave isn't the sort we needed?"

Julianne leapt on his words. "That's right. If we scout the town today, we'll at least have an idea of what we're up against. They might be able to block our magic, but we can block them, too. The attacks they've led don't seem stronger than usual, it's just those bi—those damned shields. We'll be safe, as long as we stay hidden and shielded."

Marcus narrowed his eyes as Garrett frowned. "Lass, yer skating on thin ice here. Ye know we can't shield, but ye also know we're contracted to keep ye safe."

"Perfect, then." Julianne smiled widely. "Because following us into town would be incredibly dangerous, for you and for us. Looks like it's settled: Bastian, Danil, and I will scout the town while the three of you stay back and help Annie. Well, except you, Marcus. You should rest."

Marcus looked absolutely apoplectic at that. Before his frustration could bubble over, Julianne sent him a wave of calmness.

"I might not have magic, but I can tell what you're doing," he snapped.

"Good," Julianne replied. "Because I wasn't trying to hide it. You'll need to pay the same attention if we end up taking this fight into town as a group." She stood, gathered her plates, and left the room.

As she filled the kitchen sink with water from the heavy kettle, Annie came in. She waited until Julianne was done, then cleared her throat. She twisted her apron in her hands, an uncharacteristically nervous sign.

"I just wanted to say thank you. I don't know what brought you all to these parts, but it sounds like you're at least going to try save my people. It's not much, this little village is on the edge of madness, but it's all I got."

Julianne took the old woman's hand. "I will do my very best, Annie. I'd like to ask for your help, though."

Within a few minutes, Julianne had delved through Annie's mind. She'd learned the layout of the town, the streets, the people who lived there.

She knew the farms and the buildings, the stream that cut through the center, and the shortcuts and secrets only someone who'd spent a whole life here could possibly know. She learned the faces of Annie's sons, her daughter-in-law and little Lilly, too, and left with a promise to let Annie know if she passed them on their scouting trip.

Leaving the old woman to regather her composure, Julianne went to find Danil and Bastian. The two had donned their traditional mystic robes and were pulling on their boots. "We leave soon. Bastian, can you see if there was any bread left over from breakfast? This will take us most of the day, and I don't want any mistakes made out of hunger or fatigue."

Once Bastian had left, Danil jumped in before Julianne could speak. "Are you sure we're ready for this?"

Julianne shook her head. "No, but I don't think waiting will make us any readier. It could make things worse, though. What if the New Dawn realize we're here, and why? I want this fight to be on *our* terms. Not theirs."

Danil nodded. "I'm not against the idea. Just making sure *you're* sure."

"Have I ever started something I wasn't prepared to follow through with?"

Danil pushed an image to her, of Julianne sitting close to Marcus back at camp in the Madlands. She'd been checking on his wound. Julianne watched her own silhouette as she lifted her face perilously close to Marcus's, her eyelashes lowered. When she looked at it from this perspective, it was downright seductive.

"Why, Julianne. That shade of red suits you awfully well," Danil teased.

Julianne had, indeed, flushed a vibrant shade of red. "Glad to see you're on board with the plan," she said haughtily and flounced past him. Deep down, she *was* glad. If Danil could joke about her feelings for Marcus, it meant he didn't hold it against her.

She almost tripped a step. *Wait. Did I just admit I have feelings for him?* Glad she'd been shielding Danil from her thoughts, Julianne held her head high and walked out to the stables.

Cloud Dancer nickered and nuzzled her hand. The friendly gesture made Julianne wonder if, just maybe, Bette had been right. "Sorry, girl," Julianne said. "We're going on foot today. Have to keep a low profile."

CHAPTER THIRTY

I'm ready, Bastian sent. *Unless you need me to bring anything else?*

A quick flurry of images accompanied the message, showing a couple of bread hunks wrapped in cloth and a skein of water. Julianne paled as the final image, of Bastian slipping the weapon Marcus had gifted him into his belt, crossed her vision.

Let's go, she sent, projecting that message to Danil as well. She grabbed her walking staff, left leaning against the railing of Cloud's stall, and went to meet them on the road.

"Remember," she said. "We're only going in for information. I don't want to start a fight, not without the others to back us up."

"So, we'll be going back to start a fight later?" Bastian asked.

Danil snorted then leaned past Julianne to bump Bastian's fist. Julianne raised her eyes to the heavens. "Give me strength."

They walked on for a while, trekking through the long grass by the side of the road. Though not strictly necessary, the little bit of camouflage would reduce the effort needed to avoid notice by a normal person.

If one of the New Dawn approached and was able to block them, the cover would hopefully give them time to hide. The robes served the same function. Though long seen as the uniform of the mystics and rumored to be a sign of their virtue or some rubbish, it was much simpler than that: a plain cloth was easier to 'blend' into a background than a brightly dressed person.

The rumble of a wagon made them all dive to one side. Julianne waved the others down, but sent her thoughts out towards it as it passed. A mystic, riding with a farmer. The mystic was shielded, but Julianne touched it with the gentlest of pressure. It yielded, though not enough to alert the stranger.

The wagon passed, and Julianne let out a breath.

He was shielded, but not well. No one I recognized, and I don't think he had Temple training, not as weak as he was.

Did you touch the farmer's mind? Danil's sending was grim.

No, why?

It was like working with an opium addict or an alcoholic. He was fixated on his next high, but there was a lethargy there, too. Julianne, we have *to free these people.*

Weight settled on Julianne's shoulders. He was right. No matter what, they couldn't leave these people to a life of slavery, especially under the hand of one of their own.

Julianne brushed the grass seeds off her robe, and set back off down the road. Already alert to the sounds of passers-by, it didn't take long for voices to catch her attention. The three mystics darted across the road and slowed, keeping a close eye out for anyone who might stop them.

The sounds came from a nearby orchard. The apple trees gave them enough coverage to slip closer, past the sluggish workers who probably wouldn't have noticed them even without magic.

Danil, you and Bastian wait here. I don't want us all caught in the same cage.

Danil frowned, but nodded. Julianne slipped between the trees, casting her mind wide to touch the nearby workers, then a group further afield. A short distance away, a cluster of minds congregated, emanating fear and pain. She scurried towards them.

"What the hell do you think this is? Do you think your masters, your *gods* will be happy with these takings?" The speaker was robed in blue and carried a staff much like her own. His, however, was topped with gold.

The fear increased, a desperate need to please, a terror of failing before a wrathful tyrant.

"Take them to the brewer. If nothing else, they'll get us drunk." He spat in the dirt and turned away.

Julianne pushed against the mind of the robed man before the crowd. His shield was stronger than the wagon drivers, and she debated trying to worm past it. Not worth the risk, she decided. He would probably notice the effort. She could make him forget her, but she wasn't certain that someone rifling through his mind later wouldn't notice her tampering.

Not knowing the extent of her enemy's power frustrated her to no end. Without knowing how they'd made their shields so strong, she couldn't know if that strength was reflected in other skills, like mind control, or if they even had skills Julianne hadn't seen before.

Hannah, the girl from Arcadia who'd led the charge against Adrien, had been the first in a long time to exhibit a new type of magic. Was her power a precursor to a changing system of magic?

Shaking off the ominous thought, Julianne watched a group of men cart off a wagon stacked with barrels. In the field, one of the pickers had stopped to watch. His stillness caught her eye, but she wasn't the only one to notice.

"No. No! Please, Holy Masters, please!" He winced, then writhed, dodging invisible blows. "Please, forgive me!"

The man screamed louder and Julianne's eyes prickled with tears. She knew his pain was imagined, and she knew that later, she could undo it. Now, however, she was powerless. Unless…

She reached out, not to his torturer, but to the man himself. It didn't take her long to find the intruder in his head. Ever so carefully, she slid a soft shield in place between his mind and the sensations projected into it.

Julianne diverted the illusion, giving it an ethereal quality that would buffer him from the pain. He stopped writhing and stood, tears running down his face, and wiped snot off his lip with the back of his sleeve.

He jerked as the foreign presence left his mind and Julianne quickly embedded two suggestions into his mind. First, she allowed him to see the illusion. This would alleviate the pain. He would feel it a little, but know it was false. This knowledge would protect him from the worst of it.

Less than a heartbeat later, she added the suggestion that if his torturers knew it no longer hurt, the repercussions would be terrible. The man barely blinked between the shift from agonizing pain, to relief and bewilderment, and then to a very convincing act that nothing had changed.

Julianne left his mind, satisfied his writhing screams would fool the guards, but that he was no longer suffering the pain.

Fatigue from the complicated spell made her legs weak and she slipped away, cursing her inability to help the others... yet. She was aware that she carried both Danil and Bastian in the back of her mind, and that they had seen everything she had.

You did a good thing, Danil sent.

Then why do I feel like I just left a field full of innocent people behind to suffer, while I walk away free?

Danil dropped his eyes when she returned, unwilling to meet her furious gaze. They continued down the road, this time taking less care than before.

The traffic around them increased. They first passed one villager headed into town, then another, and then a group of three. All carried packs of food or cloth, and one man dragged a small cart behind him with a table crammed into it. Each of them had a single-minded purpose: to take their gifts to their Masters.

Fields gave way to buildings and they left the main road,

taking alleys and side-passages as they slipped closer to the town center. The town was larger than Julianne had expected, despite Annie's mental images, but it was dirty and neglected.

Rubbish piled the streets and more than one house sported cracked windows. As they went, peeking in windows and ducking into doorways to avoid being seen, they picked up tiny clues.

The Masters had taken up residence in the mayor's residence. He'd been the first sacrifice, the first who they'd been unable to completely cow. That gave Julianne hope. If their other skills were as strong as their shields, they should have been able to control the mayor, though with a reasonable effort. The more you pushed a person against their nature, the harder it was to control them.

Julianne learned that many of the townspeople had fled, and that those left still had the wits to miss them. She saw the methods used, a crude combination of mind control, softening of the will, and torture mixed with lavish heaping of reward for doing as the masters wished.

A cry sent a jolt of fear through Julianne. Had they been seen?

CHAPTER THIRTY-ONE

"Find the brat! Search the houses!" Clomping feet ran through a nearby street, and Bastian grabbed Julianne's hand.

We have to go, he sent, pulling her back.

She sank her teeth into her lip, then nodded. They knew where to attack, and had a good idea of who. They could come back at night and start their assault under cover of darkness.

They ran down an alley and bolted left, using the map in Julianne's mind. Then, they reeled around as a cry sounded ahead. Turn after turn, they flitted down one street after another, only to be turned back by a searching guard or a blocked road.

The new occupants of the town didn't seem to care much about the piles of rubbish that accumulated in corners or furniture and boxes dumped in the streets. Once, a cat darted out and they froze, then retreated down another path.

Stop, Julianne said. *Forget running. We walk out.*

Julianne dipped into a trance and projected an image of them that was almost correct. Instead of dusty white robes, though, they now wore the dark cloth of the New Dawn, embellished with the insignia of the rising sun.

Bastian looked down and shook his head, looking nervous.

"Will they buy it?" he asked. "I don't think I could pull this off on my own."

Julianne winked. "You're forgetting, I did this for months. Wearing a second skin is like… well, wearing a second skin to me."

Even Danil looked doubtful, despite the crisp appearance of his robes. "You're sure you can project this illusion to anyone we pass? What if we run into someone blocked like Donna was?"

"We haven't seen anyone like that yet," Julianne pointed out. "Besides, they're looking for a child."

As one, they stepped out of the shadows. Light bounced off the gold thread at their wrists and Julianne smiled. She had crafted the image well.

They set off, almost tumbling over a small girl as they rounded a corner. She sprinted away and shot over a wall. "Lilly!" Julianne hissed, too late. She'd recognized her from the images she'd read in Annie's mind.

A scream sounded and her blood went cold.

"Got the little witch!" The victorious cry echoed off the building around them as Julianne's heart faltered.

The man cursed. A cat squealed furiously, then flew over the wall directly at Bastian. Both man and beast were equally surprised, though the cat was a lot more vocal about it. Julianne clapped a hand over Bastian's mouth until he'd extricated the feral animal's sharp claws from his robe. The animal bounded to the corner and looked back to give them a baleful hiss before disappearing.

The girl screamed again, this time a howl of anguish. "No! Temper! You hurt him, you hurt Temper! I hate—" Then she, too, fell silent.

"No…" Julianne flew to the wall and jumped.

Jules, no! Danil sent urgently.

She ignored him and hoisted herself up over the wall, just in time to see a fat, muttering member of the New Dawn stomp off with a small figure thrown over his shoulder. The tiny face was turned to one side and Julianne's heart broke. She was so young.

"He hit her," Julianne said quickly. "But she's too far away for me to wake. Come on, we have to go get her."

"Julianne!" Danil hissed, grabbing her arm. "We can come back for her. Later, with the others."

She shook him off, fury burning in her eyes. "She's a *child*, Danil. Barely seven." She looked at Bastian, the question clear on her face.

He nodded. "I'll do whatever you ask, Master."

"Thank you. We'll use our uniforms. Be ready to think fast, and have your... blasting thing ready." She gestured towards Bastian's pocket.

She turned back to Danil. "Stay clear. If a fight breaks out, you won't see clearly enough to help. This is my fight; you don't need to sacrifice yourself for it"

"To hell with that!" Danil stepped up next to her. One hand touched his forehead, then his chest in a firm salute. "You have my mind and my soul, Master."

The pledge was an old one, used whenever Selah and his council had come to a difficult decision. It was said to confirm the complete trust and loyalty the mystics had in their leader. Julianne had so far only heard it the day she took her position as Master.

Julianne blinked hard to clear her suddenly blurry vision. "Let's go then."

They set off in the direction the girl had been taken, Julianne pointedly ignoring Danil's mental query as to whether she was crying, or had just walked past a pile of rotting onions.

Because if those are *tears, I won't tell. Wouldn't want to ruin your reputation.*

You do nothing but *try to ruin my reputation.* Julianne held up a hand and they stopped, waiting until a pair of New Dawn members had passed. The couple nodded their way and the squeezing anxiety around Julianne's chest lessened a little at the confirmation the spell was working. *Seriously. I'm the leader of a Temple, and my best friend is a gambling addict?*

When the street was clear again, they headed to the right. Pinpointing the girl's location was easier now. She'd woken again, and her furious screams rang through the town.

Your best friend is a suave, mischievous bachelor who half the Temple would be tripping over themselves to get at, if they had half a brain between them.

Julianne pulled Danil around a corner and nodded at a robed figure who hurried past, ignoring them. *I didn't know Charles counted himself as my* best *friend.*

Danil pressed a hand to his chest and staggered back at the mock wound.

"I think she's in there." Julianne pointed to a small, white building ahead.

Bastian fidgeted nervously. "What's our plan? Rush them, try to take them by surprise? Or are you two just going to blind them with your dazzling wits?"

Julianne smiled. "We do what we do best. Cover me a moment."

Her eyes glowed white and her shoulders slumped. She'd need every ounce of concentration for this, and she was already, as usual, running on empty. Slipping behind the rather average mind shield held by one of the men guarding Lilly, Julianne found the information she needed. When she opened her eyes, Bastian gasped.

"Who are you?" he asked, uncertainty underlying his words.

A thin, bearded man smiled back at him with a greasy expression that made Bastian shiver. "Convincing?" Julianne asked in a strange voice, from an even stranger mouth. She smoothed her pristine navy robes and nervously pressed a hand to her new facial hair.

"Wow, Jules. I've seen you do it before, but it scares the hell out of me every time." Danil reached forwards to touch the cloth of her robe. "You know your robes are darker?"

The man—Julianne—nodded. "I am Master August. His rank is denoted by the deeper shade of blue. You two will be my aides, newly arrived in town. Shall we go?"

Bastian nodded, eyes wide. Then he shook himself and wiped the stunned expression off his face. "Yes, Master." That, at least, he could handle. It rankled him that they'd stolen the title of Master, though.

Julianne strode forwards and slammed open the door. The heavyset man jumped to attention, but not before Julianne had seen what he was doing. He'd been leaning over Lilly, who was tied to a chair and craning her neck as far as possible to get away from his warm, sticky breath.

"What the *hell* is this, Jackson?" Julianne demanded in Master August's voice.

CHAPTER THIRTY-TWO

Jackson bowed and began his stuttering explanation. "The girl, Master. I lured her in, caught her. I was just going to—"

"Lured her in? Swallow your lies. She ran straight into you. You got lucky."

Jackson nodded quickly. "Yes, Master August. Sorry, Master August." Sweat dripped off his wobbling chin and splattered onto the floor.

"Shut up, you pathetic man. Give me the girl."

"What?" Jackson's eyes darted up to his Master. "But you told me—"

"I *told* you to put a stop to her shenanigans weeks ago." That was true, according to what Julianne had seen in Jackson's memory. She had exploited his fear of his Master and his confidence of rich rewards when he handed the girl over. No better way to unsteady someone than by thwarting their expectations and turning elation to terror. "You were to contact me immediately, not sully the girl with your sweaty paws. I should have you flogged. I still might, if you forget your place again."

"Please, Master. Forgive me?" Jackson's bottom lip trembled and Julianne stifled the urge to slap him.

"Get out of my sight." The words came easily, as did the vile tone and instinctive loathing of the man. The difference was that Julianne was disgusted by what Jackson had done. August would have been disgusted at what he hadn't.

Danil and Bastian stepped forward to take Lilly's arms. She struggled and they had to hold her tightly to stop her from running. The two men half dragged, half shoved her out the door and away from her captor.

As they rounded a corner she sank her teeth into Danil's hand and he let go, cursing. Lilly snatched her other arm from Bastian's grip and tried to run, only to trip over Julianne's staff. Julianne dropped the disguises and when the girl looked up, she gasped and scrambled back against the wall.

"Shh. It's ok, Lilly. We're here to help," Julianne said.

"Who…" Lilly's eyes darted around, looking for Lord August and his two cronies.

Julianne caught her attention and, one hand on the girl's arm in case she tried to run again, stripped her fear away. Lilly sagged, then bared her teeth in defiance. Julianne raised an eyebrow at that, then slowly reassembled the image of August. Lilly's eyes grew wide and she pulled back, ready to run again. Julianne dropped the image immediately.

"Lilly, it's just a trick. A mask." Julianne reached her other hand out to Lilly and pulled the girl to her feet.

"How?" The word came out as an angry growl. Lilly scrubbed the tears from her cheeks and folded her arms across her belly.

"Mind magic. Yes, like August and his goons, but I swear we won't do anything to hurt you, Lilly."

"We can't stay here," Danil murmured to Julianne.

"We can try and sneak out." She turned to Lilly. "Or, we can use our disguises and pretend you're our prisoner."

Lilly shook her head vehemently. "Jackson *sent* for August. He wasn't surprised to see you—um, him? He was just surprised to see August *so soon*. Unless you stopped the message, he's on his way and will be here any minute. If they see you and him in the same place…"

"You're right," Julianne said. "It's too risky. I don't know that I can hide us all, though. The people we passed earlier were distracted, easy to fool. Once our ruse is discovered, they'll be hunting for us." She didn't add her other concern. If August was their leader, he was probably stronger than the lackeys he'd left to guard the town during the day. Until she met him, there was no way to tell how much stronger.

"Is there somewhere we can hide until nightfall?" Bastian asked. "It might take the heat off a little, and give us the cover of darkness when we leave."

"They were searching buildings before," Danil pointed out. "If they have all afternoon to do it, how safe do you think we'll be?"

"I want to go home."

The tiny voice made Julianne's heart break. She pulled Lilly to her, wrapping her arms around the girl. "I don't know about home just yet, but we'll get you somewhere safe."

Julianne quickly mapped their way out of the town, looping Danil and Bastian in on her plan. She gave them each an alternate route, in case they had to separate. "Whatever you do, make sure you can't be tracked back to Annie's. I don't want her pulled into this." Gripping her staff, Julianne edged towards the corner of the building. "Let's go."

They darted down the street, stopping at doorways and disappearing into shadows in between bursts of speed. Julianne gripped Lilly's hand, pulling her along as fast as the little girl could move her feet.

A loud yell sent them skittering for cover. Moments later, a voice screamed, "Find them!"

We've been made, Danil sent.

Thank you, Captain Obvious. If we're caught, take Lilly and run like hell.

Don't be an idiot. I can't protect her like you can. Danil led the charge across the street, where they stood panting for a moment before running again.

What will you do if we're separated, feel your way out of town? Just take the girl. I can do more if I don't have to worry about keeping her safe.

Danil screwed up his face and shook his head emphatically. Bastian, closed out of their conversation, watched them closely.

Julianne is right, Bastian sent. *Danil, if we get made, we have to let her do her thing.*

Stop eavesdropping, junior. How the hell did you hear that, anyway? Danil snapped at him.

I didn't. I guessed, Bastian sent. *You weren't half obvious. Julianne wants us to run while she fights. You don't want to let her, but it's the only thing that makes sense.*

Julianne rolled her eyes to the heavens. *At least someone agrees.*

They bolted down the narrow street and through an alley, then around a corner. Bastian plummeted straight into a tall woman, knocking her down. He swallowed the apology on his lips when he saw her robes.

Julianne's brain immediately kicked into gear, reaching out to silence the woman. Her probe bounced off a shield. "Oh, shit!"

"Here! I've found them! I've—" the woman screamed.

Julianne snapped a fist into the woman's face, cutting off her words. The New Dawn mystic crumpled to the ground.

"Run!" Julianne barked, and they sprinted past. They turned left, then wheeled around when they spotted two more figures at the other end of the lane.

"Here!" Julianne led them around a corner, then jerked Lilly's arm and grabbed Bastian's cuff, pulling them through a broken door. Danil threw himself in a moment later as the patrol dashed past them, oblivious to the press of bodies squashed in an abandoned cold room.

The glow in Julianne's eyes faded. "It's no good," she panted. "They're all shielded. I can't break through."

As the sounds of their hunters moved off, Danil motioned them out.

"Go through the old bakery," Lilly whispered. "I slip through there all the time."

She led them across the street, then darted a few doors down. She stopped under a dirty sign that said, *"Hank's Bread and Pastry"*. She thrust one arm through the broken glass pane and unhitched the door.

The inside of the shop smelled musty and old. A glass display case was full of green, hairy mold. Behind it, a counter sat below an opening into the kitchen behind, long but only a foot high. Motes of dust swirled past the light streaking in from the street as they moved. Bastian moved for the door beside the counter, and Lilly shook her head. He tried it anyway, but it was locked.

"This way." She climbed on the workbench behind the display case, then ducked through the opening above it.

Julianne eyed the gap. "Danil, you need to start eating less." She hopped up and followed the girl, chuckling at the grunts from Danil as he forced his way through. Bastian slipped through without a problem.

"Grownups never think of the obvious," Lilly said with a grin. She led them to the back of the room, where a strap of leather hung from a latched door. She opened it, ushered them out, then pulled it shut, making sure the end of the strap peeked through beneath. "In case I need to get in from this side," she explained.

From there, it was only two more streets to the low wall that edged the city proper. They made a run for it, easily climbing the wall and plunging into the wooded field beyond.

The trees offered some cover, but not enough. Tall trunks stretched to the sky, racing past as they ran, but branches were sparse and offered little protection. When a thick branch snapped behind them Julianne spun. Three white-eyed mystics in midnight robes dashed after them, winding through the trees, faces set with determination.

"Take the girl," Danil snapped at Bastian.

The boy looked ready to argue, but instead nodded. He grabbed Lilly and hoisted her over his shoulder, ignoring her squeak of fear. He ran, leaving Danil and Julianne to stave off their attackers.

Julianne slipped into a trance. Danil's eyes were already white, as they always were.

The three pursuers, a woman and two men, fanned out.

"Go ahead, try your little tricks." Their leader was a weedy little man, with oil slicked hair and a pointed beard. "You can't break us. We are one."

Fear spread over Julianne's face as she battered their shields. Again and again, her attacks slipped aside as they wound closer to where she and Danil stood. She pressed her back against a tree.

"How?" she asked, voice shaking. The small man sneered, and she was close enough to see his crooked, blackened tooth. "I am the Master of the Heights. You shouldn't be able to—"

As the man stepped towards her, Julianne smiled and whipped up the butt end of her walking staff. It smashed into Black Tooth's jaw. He staggered back with a howl and she jabbed it forwards again, this time slamming it into his gut.

Julianne stepped forward, still smiling. "You arrogant fool. I am a *Master*. You? You are nothing, barely a weed in the forest of my mind."

She rammed forward with the force of her mind, meeting almost no resistance from him at all. His shield was gone, shattered when his concentration failed. She spread out to find the other two were unshielded now, too. The leader collapsed, sitting down hard with glazed eyes and blood sliding down his skin from the split in his jaw. His companions stood motionless, caught in the thrall of the mystic Master.

She rifled through their minds and found it: the trick to their shields. It was a complicated spell that linked three minds, strengthening their shields via a feedback system. She let it go, knowing she wouldn't be able to replicate it without further study.

Julianne stepped up close to Black Tooth and looked down at him from above. "Tell August and whoever else will listen that a day of reckoning has come. You have one chance to leave this town. *One*. Come sunrise, I don't want to see any trace of the New Dawn except the one rising in the damned sky." She kneeled down to stare him in the eye, her white pupils reflected as points of light in the pair of muddy brown eyes. "Now, run. And don't come back."

The little man blinked as her mental suggestions took hold. Then, he began to tremble. He looked up once, quickly, before scrambling backwards. He turned, tripping as he pushed off the ground and sprinted away back towards the town.

Julianne turned to face the two remaining pursuers. "You, too."

She sent a bolt of pure, visceral terror at them. She winced when, as they turned and bolted, one slammed straight into a tree. He reeled back, blood streaming from his nose below terrified eyes, and staggered off as fast as he could.

"You couldn't have planned *that* any better," Danil said. "If it didn't look so damn painful, that would have been hilarious."

"We need to go," Julianne said in a low voice. She took Danil's arm, and together they ran to find Bastian and Lilly.

Julianne let Danil lead, using her eyes and his memory. He had stayed connected with Bastian as he'd fled with Lilly, and his practice at navigation gave him a good idea of which way to go. Fast and silent, they darted through the trees, then plummeted down an embankment.

"Danil!" Julianne gasped as his hand slid from hers. They slid down the short hill, landing in a heap at the bottom.

Panting and cursing, they lay for a moment. Julianne reached out with her mind and found Bastian, who appeared above her a moment later.

"This way. We've found a place to hide until nightfall."

CHAPTER THIRTY-THREE

He led them along the bottom of the embankment to a section that formed a hollow in the dirt. Ferns grew at the lip above, trailing down to cover the space. Pushing aside the branches, Julianne crept in to sit beside Lilly. The girl's eyes glowed, not the white of a mystic, but green.

A bird called overhead and her eyes cleared. "Tarchus said they didn't follow," she said, matter-of-factly. "Master August is calling his guards back in. They're stopping the search."

"It's too soon," Julianne murmured. "Why would they give up so quickly?"

Danil shrugged. "Maybe they just don't care. Or, maybe he's fortifying the town, doesn't want his people spread out in case of an attack."

"Oh, there'll be an attack." Julianne's voice was hard. Her eyes glowed white. "There are people, but not close. How long can we stay here unseen?"

"Go that way," Lilly said. She pointed further along the furrow in the ground to where leafy ferns had taken root.

They crawled over. Leaves reached out to form a small, green refuge. Lilly pressed her hand on the ground and her eyes lit up again as tiny, curled fronds unfurled to extend the foliage and thicken it.

"Thank you, Lilly. You're very talented." Julianne's heart went out to the little girl. "What were you doing in the town? Have you been there all along?"

Lilly shrugged. "Mostly out here, in the trees. I'm good at hiding. Escaping, too. That's not the first time they caught me, I always get away." Then, her chin trembled. "Not the first time they hurt one of my friends, either."

"Temper?" Julianne asked gently.

Lilly nodded. "He's my favorite. He doesn't like people, and neither do I."

"He sounds like a pretty clever cat," Danil whispered. "And you sound like a pretty clever kid. I bet he's already found a nice warm place to curl up by now."

Lilly seemed to accept this. The corners of her mouth lifted in a wavering smile. "Next time, he'll claw the bastard's eyes out."

Julianne darted a glance at the girl. Nope, she really did look that young. Julianne reminded herself that even she had learned salty language by that age, and this girl had gone through a lot more than she had.

The low rumble of distant hoofbeats caused a sharp intake of breath from all of them, but they passed by without stopping. They sat in silence, watching the shadows lengthen. Julianne allowed herself to drop into a light meditation, keeping her senses alert for anyone approaching.

When the sun finally painted the sky in hues of purple, she roused herself. Lilly had fallen asleep, her small body tucked in next to Julianne for warmth. Tenderness rushed through her as she gently rubbed the girl's arms to wake her.

"We need to go, Lilly."

They shook off the dirt and twigs and traipsed through the pine forest, back towards the road. Despite the cloud-covered darkness, they kept to the long grass. Lilly gripped Julianne's hand tightly and shoved at the tickling blades, trying to keep them away from her face.

"Lilly," Bastian whispered. "How about a ride?" He leaned down and gestured to his back, and Lilly's eyes lit up.

She looked to Julianne for permission, then raced over and climbed onto his shoulders.

Is that wise? Danil sent to Julianne. *The whole point of the grass was to hide us.*

Hush, Danil. The poor child is exhausted and these reeds are as tall as she is. She was making a valiant effort, but she was struggling.

Danil walked on, surer footed in the darkness than Julianne was. Ahead, Bastian seemed to have no issue with the uneven ground, loping along as if Lilly weighed no more than a feather.

"Do you hear that?" Danil asked.

"Hoofbeats," Julianne confirmed.

Lilly slid off Bastian's shoulders and dove into the brush, Bastian close behind her. Julianne was about to throw herself in when Danil grabbed her arm, a fierce grin lighting his face.

Julianne reflexively reached out with her mind, and had to scrub tears of relief from her eyes when she immediately recognized Bette and Garrett.

"Over here," Danil called, as the pair almost flew straight past them, leading two spare horses.

"Thank the Bitch in all her glory," Bette breathed, pulling her horse to a halt. "Marcus would have had our heads if we'd had to go back without ye. The lad's downright beside himself with worry."

Julianne gave a brief explanation of their trip, and introduced Lilly. By the time she'd finished, Bastian had mounted Lilly on one of the horses and the girl was lying over its neck whispering to it, eyes as green as a casting mystic's glowed white.

"We only brought two spare nags, thinking Bette and I could share the one, and the three of ye would have one each left. I suppose Cloud could carry both Julianne and the wee girl. She looked like she'd not weigh more than a leaf." Garrett looked to Bette for confirmation.

"I'll ride with him." Lilly pointed at Bastian. "This is his horse. She doesn't like the way he rides, but I can show him how to make her comfortable."

Garrett gaped. "Ahh. I dinna think the old beast can carry ye both, child."

"Oh, she can," Lilly said confidently. "She said his legs are long, but he's not all hard muscle like you and Bette. She likes Bette most, though."

Bette barked a laugh. "The girl knows. Go on, close yer mouth, rearick, and climb yer horse. Lilly, can young Duster here hoist both me and Garrett?"

Lilly shrugged. "He's strong, but he thinks you'd be better to let the blind one ride with the lady. Her horse—Cloud Leaper? She's carried them both and said she's happy to again. She wants to get moving, though. It's late and she thinks it's silly to be outside when you could be in a nice, warm stable." Lilly punctuated her words with a yawn.

After a few raised eyebrows and a quick reshuffle, Bastian mounted up behind Lilly, and they set off. She showed him how to move his legs and relax his posture while the others caught up. "There, that's better. You must have been awfully uncomfortable riding like that."

Bastian groaned. "You've no idea." He still had aches in muscles he didn't know existed.

"That girl is certainly one of a kind," Danil said into Julianne's ear.

"She's strong. Not just her magic—I can't judge a druid's power, but I think she may have some real talent there. But to stay in the town, hiding from those awful men for so long?"

Danil murmured his agreement. "She needs training. Perhaps we could organize something."

They pushed the horses to make the journey home a short

one. Lilly insisted on helping Garrett rub them down, leaving Bette to announce their return to a very impatient Marcus.

"What happened? You found them? Was anyone hurt?" he demanded.

"Lots, about a mile down the road, and no." Julianne answered his rapid-fire questions in order as she entered the house, Danil at her heels.

"The situation in town is worse than we expected," Danil added. "The New Dawn have enslaved basically the whole village, using mental magic as both punishment and reward. They're working them into the ground."

"The people we found were in a pitiful state, working their fingers to the bone for nothing but a false sense of happiness." Julianne chewed at her lip, remembering the man who had taken the flogging. "They're broken, Marcus."

"Will they help us fight?" Marcus asked.

Julianne shook her head. "There's no way to tell. Even if we could break whatever spell holds them, they've been tortured and starved. They could be itching to fight back, or past the point of wanting to." Julianne cursed herself for not seeking the answer to the mind control tactic when she had the New Dawn members under her spell.

"Looks like it's up to us, then. That is, if you're intent on seeing this through?"

"I don't have a choice, Marcus. You should have seen—" Julianne bit her words off as Lilly walked inside.

"Where's Annie?"

"Lilly? Child, where have you been hiding? I hadn't heard from you in days, I was worried sick," came Annie's voice.

"Annie!" Lilly threw herself into the old woman's arms and burst into tears. "Annie, they hurt Temper! They made him run away." Her words fell to pieces as she sobbed against the old woman's chest.

"Oh, Lilly. You poor thing. That crotchety old beast will come back just as soon as his belly starts to rumble; you take my word for it." Annie patted the girl's hair, her eyes closed against the pain unleashed in the safety of her arms.

Tears sprang to Julianne's own eyes. The girl had shielded her emotions so savagely, not even the Mystic Master had realized the depth of her anguish.

"Lilly… I'm so sorry. If I'd known, I'd have gone back for him."

Red, puffy eyes stared blankly up at Julianne. ""Why? He wouldn't talk to you, you're just a human." Lilly's voice cracked on the last word, and she buried her face back into Annie's shirt.

Julianne ached to strip Lilly of her grief, to numb her pain and flood her with soothing comfort. She did not. Humans had a tremendous capacity to withstand grief and pain. Doing so was how growth was attained. Empathy, strength, love. All could spring from a hurt so terrible that it felt like it would choke the soul dry.

Instead, Julianne reached her mind out to touch her surroundings. The instant connection with the universe soothed her own roughened nerves and dulled the throbbing grief that pulsed through the room.

Waves of emotion passed through her. Sadness, for the dead mystics at the Temple all those weeks ago, for Annie's sorrow over her missing sons, for Temper, and for a little girl who shouldn't be worrying about more than dolls and play dates.

Frustration, at the blocking spell that had thwarted her attempts to stop Donna and see her plans, at not knowing who here could do the same, at not having a plan.

Finally, anger. A righteous fury blossomed in Julianne's breast. This corruption was born of a magic she lived and breathed, one she had studied for most of her life, one she had dedicated her every heartbeat to.

The New Dawn had taken what was once pure, something made of kindness and empathy and a living connection with the universe, and perverted it. They'd twisted it into a tool to oppress instead of help, to enslave instead of liberate.

Julianne let that weight settle inside her, let it coalesce into a tiny ball. It shrank until it was no bigger than a pinhead, compressing and straining under the pressure.

The New Dawn had done this.

The New Dawn was going down.

CHAPTER THIRTY-FOUR

After the house was quiet, Julianne, Annie, and Marcus sat at the rickety old kitchen table. Julianne gripped a mug of hot tea, untouched. Annie stood and reached into a nearby cupboard. When she unscrewed the bottle of brandy and dumped a slug into Julianne's cup, the mystic simply smiled.

"Thank you, Annie. I don't doubt I'll be needing that by the end of the night."

"Julianne, you can't really mean to attack them directly?" Marcus nodded at Annie as she waggled the bottle in front of him, and gratefully accepted the glass. "You have no idea how many there are, how they're armed; you don't even know how strong their magic is."

"You said it yourself, Marcus. I can't walk away from this; I have to see it through." Julianne sipped from her cup, then closed her eyes as blissful warmth tingled through her body. "I do have one trick up my sleeve, though. I figured out how they can shield so strongly. I can't do it myself, not yet, but all it takes is to distract one of their circle to break them all."

"This is crazy, Jules. I thought you meant you'd go for help, not dive into the hornet's nest! Maybe Amelia can send in a patrol from Arcadia. I know there's not many she can trust, but she might be able to do this. And what about your mystic friend?" Marcus's eyes were slightly wide, evidence of his worry in his creased brows.

Julianne shook her head. "Amelia has her own problems to worry about. And anyway, a patrol would take far too long to organize. As for Artemis, we don't even know where he is, or if he could or even would help us."

"Oh, he'd help alright," Annie said. "He might be odd, but he's no coward."

"Regardless," Julianne cut in. "He isn't here. Unless you know something we don't?" A tendril of hope flared at the chance Artemis might participate in the fight.

Annie shook her head sadly. "If I knew where he was, I'd tell you."

The tiny spark of hope died. "Well, then. It's just us. Well," she looked at Marcus, "not you."

"What?" Marcus's eyes snapped brightly.

Julianne shrugged. "You're injured. You can't swing a sword, draw a bow, or throw a hammer. I know you have your magitech, but you can't rely on that alone. It does damage, but the range isn't there. By the time they got close enough for it to be effective, you'd be fighting for them."

Marcus sputtered. "I'm your best fighter, even injured!"

"So… you really think you're up to it?" Julianne leaned across the table, brows furrowed.

Marcus nodded eagerly. "I'll have to watch the wound, sure. Don't want to split it open again. But it's a shallow cut, and there's no trace of infection thanks to Annie's salve."

Annie nodded at that.

"Fine. Annie, I don't want you and Lilly here tomorrow, just in case they trace us back here. I'm so sorry to have to ask you to do this, but is there somewhere safe you can go for a little while?"

Annie snorted. "I know this whole region like my own backyard. There's some caves a little way north; the hunters used to stay there when they were off collecting furs. Now that winter's broken, it won't be too uncomfortable for the girl, and I'm tough old bones. It'll be fine, dear. You go do your thing and don't you worry about us."

Julianne breathed a sigh of relief, glad that the old woman and the Druid child wouldn't be caught in the crossfire. "Thank you, Annie."

Together, the three sketched out a map of the town, marking key locations where the higher-ranking mystics would likely be found. August was rumored to have taken up in the old Lord's manor on the southern side of the city. Julianne's preference was to attack there first, to try and take out the head of the serpent.

Marcus pursed his lips, thinking. Her plan was solid. It would avoid fighting in the streets, an act that was likely to have them surrounded in moments. They'd be able to take down the leader and search his apartments for information on the rest of the Dawn, then flee before being discovered. They could make more plans from there.

"No, Marcus." Julianne interrupted his train of thought, reaching out to grab his arm urgently. "This isn't a reconnaissance mission. We finish this today."

Her eyes flashed with determination, and he knew it was a fight he wouldn't win. Marcus groaned. "You really don't know what you're in for," he said. "But, it's your choice. I'm just along for the ride."

"Go get some sleep," she said. "We all should. It's past midnight, and we need to leave before dawn."

CHAPTER THIRTY-FIVE

A tiny hand shook Julianne awake. She blinked her eyes and squinted into the darkness before reaching out with her mind to the small figure sitting on her bed. She groggily reached out to Lilly's thoughts. Seeing the urgency there, Julianne shot up.

"Marcus!" she yelled. "Bette, Garrett, get up."

The house exploded into action as lamps were lit and people tumbled out of bed, grabbing weapons and swearing as they looked around for the threat. Marcus shoved past the door, into Julianne's room.

"What is it?" he asked, eyes quickly taking in the dazed rearick, and the mystic still tucked under her blankets next to Lilly.

"Marcus, the New Dawn are on their way. I need you to take Lilly and Annie somewhere safe."

Anger and frustration boiled under Marcus's skin. "No! We talked about this. You can't send me away, Julianne."

She touched his face and opened her mind. She let him see her true self, her care for him, and her worry about his safety. Then, she led him into her mind as Master. Here, she thought of pragmatism.

Even with all emotion removed from the equation, she knew Marcus was the best person to lead the civilians to safety, that Bette and Garrett would fight better together than if they were separated, that she needed Danil and Bastian, but also needed to know someone she trusted was looking after the innocent people caught in a war that had nothing to do with them.

Worry stabbed at Marcus's chest, but he nodded. "Fine. I'll take them somewhere safe, but as soon as I can, I'll return to help."

"That's all I ask of you," Julianne said. Her heart brimmed with gratitude, but her soul was crippled with worry for him.

He turned to go, but she caught his hand, jerking him back to her. She pulled him down and stared into his green flecked eyes. "Stay safe, soldier. I mean it."

Then, she kissed him, long and deep. All the pent-up emotion inside her flowed through it, the pain and the passion and frustration not only of their task, but of being so close to him for so long.

Marcus pulled back, panting for breath and trembling a little.

"Now go," Julianne instructed. She stepped past him and spoke to Garrett. "I'm fairly certain I know how their shields work. I needed you and Bette to help me disable them. Get dressed, we have less than an hour before they get here."

"I…" Marcus looked around the room, still dazed.

"Ye heard the Master, ye love-struck fool. Get goin'!" Bette chided. She gave Marcus a gentle push that seemed to shake him out of it. He strode out, calling for Annie.

"Lilly, is Tarchus still flying over them?" The image that passed from the bird to the girl—and then to Julianne—had showed a column of dark-robed people marching down the road in their direction. They were led by a figure whose golden robes almost twinkled in the moonlight. That one had made them both shudder. "Don't tell me. Just think it, and I'll know."

Julianne had tried reading the bird's mind through Lilly's

mind, but it was like trying to decipher a foreign language. However, as soon as Lilly translated the images, Julianne had a clear picture.

Julianne saw the road she'd walked the day before, but from above. The mystics were on the very outskirts of the farms, marching behind their leader in two lines towards Annie's house, flanked by a column of plainly dressed fighters on either side, armed with swords and cudgels. The road ran to her door; the only thing past it was the Madlands, and even Danil wouldn't bet against that being their destination.

She watched as the bird idly drifted lower and noticed an abnormality in the formation. Three of the group was too close together, instead of evenly spaced like the rest. *Lilly, can Tarchus see what's happening at the end of that second row?*

Tarchus waited a moment, then directed his laser focus where Julianne had requested. He didn't need to fly closer—his sight was incredibly good. He just had to look right at them. It only took a second for him to pick out the ropes that bound their wrists and ankles.

The top-down view gave little impression of their faces, but when one of the three wiped his face on his sleeve, tilting his head for barely a moment, Julianne immediately recognized his slicked hair and sculpted beard.

Black tooth, Julianne thought, forgetting to shield the thought from Lilly.

"He's as bad as the fat one," Lilly said. "They're all bad, but those two especially, and her." An image accompanied her words of a woman with abnormally red hair and lines about her eyes.

"Donna was here?" Julianne asked.

"Yes. They call her the Master's Voice. We haven't seen her for a while, though." Lilly's face screwed up ferociously. "I hope she's dead."

Julianne recognized the tone and odd phrasing as a thought

not of Lilly's own, but something repeated. Aloud, she asked, "Who is the leader we saw just now? The one in gold?"

Lilly shrugged. "August, probably. He's the only one I've seen in dark blue. Fatso caught me once before, said August would string me up by my toenails and make me kill all my pets. Said he'd make me like it, too."

The hard pebble inside Julianne flared, just slightly, imagining what had been said to the young girl. "Don't worry, Lilly. We won't let them take you again."

Marcus reappeared and hustled the girl out of the room. "Have you got everything? Quick, run downstairs and wait with Annie. I'll be there in a moment."

Suddenly alone with Marcus, Julianne let her eyes fall. She didn't know what had come over her earlier. Maybe a residual effect of the remnant? No. She knew that wasn't true.

"Marcus, we don't have time for any of this. I just didn't want you to go without…"

"I understand." He stepped forwards and folded her in his arms, a brief hug that was over all too soon.

"Stay safe," Julianne whispered. "And keep them safe, too. Someone has to survive this mess… in case I don't."

Marcus squeezed her arm, then left without another word.

CHAPTER THIRTY-SIX

Julianne stood at Annie's front door, waiting. The visitors were close enough to sense now. She ran her mind over the soldiers, all controlled by mental force. Their shields weren't as strong as the mystics, but for now, they were enough.

Her mental magic caressed the two columns of men, slipping over the tightly shielded space between them. At this distance, she was virtually powerless except for her ability to touch them. Soon, though…

Julianne reached out to her comrades. Danil and Bastian were a short distance away. They would join the fight last, after Julianne dismantled the shields they used and freed the farmers turned soldiers. They would be their second line of defense, turning against their keepers once the bonds of slavery were loosened.

That was the hope, anyway. She was working on a theory and a feeling, something that didn't often lead her wrong but could have devastating consequences tonight.

There's always a first time, she thought to herself. Julianne took the last few moments of quiet to ease into a short meditation. She bathed in the connectedness, reaching out to touch the universe around her.

The old timbers in the house groaned with anticipation, and the leaves outside rustled excitedly. Julianne could almost feel the heartbeat of the world flutter with anxiety.

Then, it happened. A flare of consciousness off in the distance. One of the mystics had slipped in their control of a guard, releasing the shield just long enough for Julianne to slip beneath it.

Quickly, she read the man's recent memories. Tarik had been dragged from his bed, ensorcelled into obeying despite an injury in his shoulder. He and the other men had quickly donned armor and weapons and marched out of the town to await their masters.

They'd been given no rest and no explanation. That didn't matter. Tarik's only desire was to obey, any semblance of resistance long since stripped by constant cycles of fear and reward.

When Julianne estimated they were only a half-mile down the winding path, she struck. Blasting through Tarik's mind control link, she replaced it with her own.

Before applying any force, she sent a simple question.

Are you willing?

Tarik twitched his head, dazed.

These monsters, those who call themselves Master. They killed your people. Took you as a slave. Will you stand for that?

She watched as his mind slowly woke.

Who are you? He wondered. *Have I gone mad? Did they finally break my mind?*

Do you feel broken, or do you feel ready to fight? Julianne asked him. *Are you willing to sacrifice yourself for the freedom of others?*

When he straightened his shoulders and gripped his spear tighter, she felt it. *These bastards took my people. I am* willing.

He surrendered his will to her, allowing her full control of his body. The New Dawn guards were nothing but a show. They had all the power they needed to control the population in their minds.

Though a strong man, his only experience fighting had been with obstinate sheep on shearing and dipping days. Julianne, however, had spent months with the Arcadian guards.

She used his body like a weapon, harnessing a strength she personally didn't have. The spear he carried whipped out at the head of the nearest mystic, taking him down in a single blow. The woman next to him screamed, the blood spatter on her face black in the moonlight.

Pain blossomed in Julianne's shoulder as she felt his arm dislocate from the socket at the force of the blow. Ahh, that was the injury. She pushed the sensation away.

A guard stabbed forward with a sword but Julianne pulled Tarik back, and he missed. Holding the spear out between them defensively, Julianne feinted once. The farmer flinched, then lunged, only to take the brunt of Tarik's head straight into his nose.

Julianne's head rang as she suffered the same sensations as Tarik. She let out a scream as she plunged him into the center of the scrambling mystics, swinging the cudgel left, then right, then jabbing it forwards into someone's belly. A blow struck him from behind, but Julianne forced him back to his feet, dropping the weapon from blood slicked hands.

Tarik reached out for the nearest mystic and wrapped his fingers around her neck. He squeezed, life flowing from his wounds as his consciousness faded.

Thank you, my friend. Julianne watched through his eyes as the woman fell in a heap, and as all went dark, felt the thud of Tarik's body following. *Your sacrifice was noble and brave. Your people will know you as their hero.* As his soul dissipated, Julianne pushed a wave of loving calm to send him on his way.

A disconnected part of her mind searched the army as they wailed and yelled. Three were dead—four including Tarik—and the shields of seven mystics were shattered. As Julianne tried to force herself into one of them, she was suddenly shoved back as their defenses snapped shut. Three had re-fortified themselves, but four were wide open, or at least had flimsy shields erected that Julianne would be able to breeze past.

Alec! Desiree, link with me!

Please, no, don't shut me out!

Julianne watched as they scrambled, three of the vulnerable mystics grabbing hands as their eyes regained their white glow. She sat inside the mind of Trini, a narrow-faced woman who sneered as the man who held her hand kicked another mystic who begged to be joined to them.

"Don't be an idiot, Henry. It only works with three." Trini seethed, sick of having to deal with these idiots. If not for them holding her back, she knew she'd be at Master August's side by now.

Unwilling to make herself known just yet, Julianne used her magic to feel her way along the woman's mind. Though she couldn't sense the magic another person cast, it was never magic alone. A whispered word, a mental image, a feeling—all that and more could accompany a spell.

What Julianne felt was a reluctant surrender, a stepping back as Trini allowed another inside her head as she built her shield. Julianne could tell Trini wasn't happy with the process. She felt the men she worked with were beneath her, unworthy of touching her superior mind.

Julianne pulled back as far as she could without losing contact, staying as still and quiet as she could.

Trini's consciousness separated as she entered the minds of two others. The shield strengthened, wavered, and fell.

"Concentrate, you idiots," Trini snapped.

"It's not us, you dumb cow. It fell apart at your link."

Julianne's mind raced. If what they were doing only worked

with three minds, as they'd told poor old Henry, it was likely her presence that held them back.

She had learned as much as she could without exposing herself, and it was all she needed. Julianne send a tendril of frustration into Trini's mind, feeding her anger at the men beside her. Fanning it, Julianne nudged Trini towards the small knife she kept in her belt.

Julianne exploded fury inside Trini's mind, and the New Dawn woman grabbed the weapon. It had been a gift from Trini's father, more ornament than a real weapon. Still, when Trini thrust it into Henry's cheek, it did the job.

Julianne increased the pressure on the woman's mind. Trini held the short knife pointed at her own stomach.

No. No, please.

Julianne planted her resolve, pushing against the other woman's desire to live. Too far for direct control, Julianne dragged up the image of the man she'd just stabbed, flooding Trini with guilt.

She barely responded. Gritting her teeth, Julianne searched the woman's mind, trying to find her motivation. There. Trini was ambitious, proud, and shallow. She was also fearful. The people she was involved with were harsh masters and dealt out punishments like candy.

Trini fought against the terror that built as images of those punishments flashed through her mind. "No, no… They wouldn't, not to me." she murmured. The words were a lie. She was now a weak link, a gaping wound. The only thing they could do to fix that wound was to cauterize it.

They would not do so kindly. Trini sobbed, then plunged the knife between her ribs. A painful death, but a fast one. A kinder one than she'd have been given if she'd survived this battle and made it back to her people.

Julianne slipped away as it pierced, bubbles filled Trini's lungs. She had missed the heart; it would not be a peaceful death.

Bastian, Danil, do what you can to break their shields. They operate in groups of three—take one down, two more will follow.

How? Bastian asked. *While they're up, they're impenetrable.*

Think about what makes you lose focus. Do that to them, one hundredfold. Julianne sent the image of a tapestry that hung in the initiates dorms. It showed a woman, hand out, warding off anger, fear, fatigue and pain. The four symbols defined the things most difficult to overcome when using mental magic.

So... piss them off, make them cry, wear them down, then punch them, Bastian sent. *Got it.*

Jules? Danil's sending held a note of caution.

There are two exposed. You and Bastian need to take them. I'll give the rearick a heads up and take a moment to gather myself.

Danil replied with a jab of warning and Julianne took it to heart. She'd used a dangerous amount of energy already, and the fight had barely begun.

She ducked away from the door and signaled to Bette, who was hidden outside by a window. Julianne scurried over and whispered instructions to her.

"Cause as much havoc as you can. Ten wounded is better than two dead. Once they lose focus, their shields go down in groups of three."

"Aye. Shoot many, shoot well. I like the sound of that." Bette grinned and ducked back down, darting off through the shadows towards Garrett by the barn.

CHAPTER THIRTY-SEVEN

"Wait," Lilly called from behind Marcus.

He turned, ready to scoop the girl up and carry her if need be. Instead of the tired child he expected to see, though, Lilly stood tall, her eyes sparkling with green light.

The bushes nearby trembled and Marcus tensed.

"Easy, boy. Girl knows what she's doing." Annie touched his arm reassuringly and then gripped tighter when a large bear ambled onto the goat track they followed.

Marcus sucked in a hissing breath when it approached the child. Instead of running or cowering, she grinned. "Thank you, Snuffy."

"Snuffy?" Marcus asked, heart still racing.

"I don't know how to say his bear name with words. Snuffy suits him, though. He likes to smell things."

As if to prove her words, Snuffy rose on his back feet and sniffed at the air. Then he dropped back down, and Lilly climbed on his back. "It's ok. He won't hurt you. He said he'll carry me a little way, but he doesn't like people. He'll go before we get there."

Wondering how things had gotten so weird so fast, Marcus looked at Annie. "Get where?"

At least the old woman had the decency to look abashed. "Some secrets just aren't mine to tell," she said.

They walked on, their progress made faster by the heavy animal that forged ahead, snapping stray branches to clear the path for Marcus and Annie.

"Was she always like this?" Marcus asked Annie quietly.

She nodded. "Goddess blessed her early. Even as a kit, the animals looked to her. She'd walk through the forest attracting the biggest beasts around, and not a one ever hurt her."

"Seems like a handy gift to have," Marcus said.

"True. Until you're damn near run out of town by those who are jealous or don't understand. People round these parts might worship Queen Bethany Anne, but damned if they don't pick and choose how they apply her teachings."

"So, you believe the Queen Bitch is a Goddess?"

Annie nodded. "Oh, not like in those kids' fairy tales. We're backwater, but we're not stupid. Still, seems sure enough Bethany Anne had something to do with the gifts that appear every now and then, if the stories had even a grain of truth to them."

"Huh." Marcus pushed a branch out of his way before it snapped back in his face.

When Marcus looked back up, he saw Snuffy had stopped. Raising his head, the bear sniffed again, hackles raising as he let out a low, menacing rumble.

"Lilly?" Marcus called in a low voice. "You need to get down."

Lilly shook her head, face pale. "No. Snuffy said I'm safer up here. He said I have to hang on, though."

"Hang on to what?" Marcus asked.

Before Lilly could answer, three remnant dropped from the forest canopy above. One landed on Marcus, sending his weapon flying down the embankment beside him. He kicked hard and the remnant thumped back to the ground.

It sprang to its feet faster than Marcus could. He scrambled backwards, keeping an eye on the bush his magitech device had caught in. If he could just get down there…

A body flew across the path, tumbling into the remnant that bore down on Marcus. He darted a look back just in time to see Snuffy thump back down onto all fours, Lilly clinging to the thick fur on his back.

The bear whipped his head to one side and let out a screaming roar, spittle flying at the remnant Annie was warding off with a thick branch. The bear lunged, taking the remnant's head in its giant mouth. He shook it like a playful dog.

After the remnant's body had flown into the bushes, Snuffy casually dropped the soggy head from his mouth. He looked to Marcus and flared his nostrils angrily.

Marcus, now sure the bear did Lilly's bidding, looked behind him. The remnant that had tumbled into the brush was right behind him. It was holding his weapon, but like a spear instead of a shooting weapon.

Marcus dodged the first attack, ducking as the remnant swung the magitech staff. He looked up as something cracked above him and almost lost his head to Annie's tree branch. The remnant was halfway down the slope before Marcus realized what had happened.

"Damn, Annie, you've got one hell of an arm on you."

"What do you expect?" she called down after him as he went after the remnant. "I raised two boys with no Pa to teach them how to play catch."

Marcus found the fallen remnant. It staggered back up the hill, clearly dazed by the blow to its head. Marcus had no trouble dispatching it with his boot knife. On his way back, he spotted the magitech weapon and picked it up, sighing in relief as he hefted its weight in his hand.

Marcus nodded thanks to Annie as he reached them. "You ok up there, Lilly?" he called.

"We're ok," she called back, leaning down to cuddle the bear. "Snuffy kept me safe. He doesn't like the mad people."

"Err... Thank you, Snuffy," Marcus said warily. He gave the bear a halfhearted wave.

"He said you're welcome." She paused, eyes glowing green as she frowned. "Well, why didn't you tell me that? Silly old bear." Her eyes cleared. "One of the mad people bit Snuffy on his front paw. He said it's not very bad, but it does hurt. We might have to slow down a bit."

Marcus looked at the bear, whose beady black eyes watched him closely. He warred with himself for a moment, then heaved a sigh. "Will Snuffy let me look at it? Those bites can go septic pretty quickly."

The bear lifted a paw and Marcus saw it was matted with wet blood. He dribbled some water over it from his flask.

"Here," said Annie. She handed him a small tin box. It reeked of the stuff Bette had dressed his wounds with earlier.

Tamping down the fear and nerve, Marcus explained to Lilly that he wanted to apply some cream to the injury, then bind it. The girl's eyes lit up again as she relayed the instructions, then nodded for Marcus to begin.

He'd never doctored a bear before, but he soon realized that with Lilly's firm hand to guide it, his patient was better behaved than some of the soldiers he'd worked with.

Once he was done, Snuffy gingerly dropped his paw to the ground and tested his weight on it. Apparently satisfied, he bumped Marcus's hand with his nose.

"Uh, you're welcome?" he said hesitantly.

"I think he likes you," Lilly giggled.

They kept on for another hour, their pace a little slower, but still faster than Lilly could have walked on her own. Eventually, the bear stopped again, sniffed, and slowly stood up.

"What is it?" Marcus asked, slipping into a defensive stance and looking around.

"Nothing's wrong," Lilly said as she slid down' Snuffy's back. "We're close now. Snuffy can't come any further, or they'll get scared."

"Scared? Who?" Marcus looked to Annie for an answer, but she just tapped the side of her nose.

Stifling his frustrated curiosity, Marcus let Annie take the lead. She called out a terse thank you to Snuffy for his services, then stalked ahead.

Marcus trotted to catch up as she disappeared around a bend. He stepped around the corner then stopped dead in his tracks.

"What the *fuck?*"

CHAPTER THIRTY-EIGHT

Julianne stood at Annie's front door, resisting the urge to send her mind wandering towards the enemy again. It would be easier to work once they were in view, and she needed to save her energy.

Julianne meditated, drawing back the energy she'd used. When a scream echoed through the night, she blew out a slow breath. Killing was anathema to mystics, but sometimes, it was needed.

To take a guilty life in order to protect an innocent one was a burden she was willing to bear, as many times as it took to free the people her magic had enslaved. She reminded herself of that as the sound of the enemy drew near.

"To arms!" Julianne screamed, using magic to echo her voice to sound like an army. It wouldn't affect the shielded mystics, but the mind-controlled guards would be squirming in their boots. The less they wanted to comply, the greater effort the mystics would have to expend to keep them under control. And, she thought with a smile, the greater the chance the guards would begin to break free.

Her cry signaled the rearick, and the quiet sound of running feet let her know Bette, at least, was on her way.

An arrow flew through the air, aimed at the corner the army would round in just a few moments. Three more flew before a muttered *scheisse* sounded from the trees.

Steady on, Julianne thought. She didn't send the words, too focused on the empty road.

Surrenderrrrr. The word whispered through her mind like a gentle breeze. Julianne gripped her staff tighter. Then, Bette screamed.

CHAPTER THIRTY-NINE

Annie stood proudly in the center of the small crowd that had gathered beneath the rocky overhang. Beside it, an open clearing was dotted with small tents and basic buildings.

"Don't look so insulted, boy. I told you, it wasn't my secret to tell. These people fled for their lives, nearly all of them are weak and vulnerable and couldn't stand up to those cretins down in the village. I couldn't break their trust, not even for your pretty girlfriend."

Marcus blushed. "She's not my girlfriend."

"What have you brought us, Annie?" A burly man stepped forward from the small group of refugees. He leaned heavily on a walking stick.

"Settle yourself, Hank. He's part of the group I sent word about. Turns out, they're not a bit like those twats that took our town. They're here to help."

Hank frowned, putting himself between Marcus and the women and children behind him. "How do we know you won't just take their place? Small town like ours is just ripe for the picking."

"You trying to give him ideas, Hank?" an old woman called from behind him.

"I'm just stating what any fool can see with their own eyes."

"Please, just hear me out." Marcus put his hands up defensively. "Julianne is the leader of a colony of mystics, from across the Madlands. A few weeks ago, a woman named Donna turned up, spewing hate and saying she and her friends wanted to take over the whole damn world."

Marcus scanned the faces before him. Some had started at Donna's name. Others simply nodded with recognition. "Julianne refused to let that happen. She'd just risked everything to save Arcadia from the same fate, from Adrien's rule." Now, they looked blank, confused. He screwed up his face, wishing she were here to help him talk to these people.

"Look, Adrien was a bad guy, ok? He had magic and used it to push people into the dirt, elevate himself above them. Julianne was part of the revolution that took him down."

"She saved a bunch of these mystic people from a dictator?" Hank asked.

"No." Marcus took a deep breath. "She saved people like you. Well, like you, but piss poor and crammed into an overpopulated slum. Adrien created that slum, forced the people into it and took what money they had so they had no hope of getting out."

"And your woman took his head off?"

Marcus smirked. "Not alone. But she was there, fighting for the people when it happened. So was I. And we won't stand by and let another self-righteous dictator ruin lives. Now, who wants to take some heads?"

"I never can tell. Did you mean than in a literal sense?" Another old man stepped forward, his matted hair swinging down past his elbows and his beard almost as long—and disgusting. He noticed Marcus's grimace and snorted. "You'd look like shit, too, if you were living in a damned cave for this long. Gah, the manners of some people." He turned away irritably, and it was only then that a shocked Marcus had realized what was different about the old man.

Not his tattered shirt or gnarled fingers. Not the coating of grime. His eyes. His eyes were white as snow.

CHAPTER FORTY

Julianne swallowed hard, but didn't rush forward. Instead she carefully reached out, finding Bette still in the trees unharmed. A trick, and a lousy one at that. Julianne strengthened her shields and stepped back into the shadows. She threw her mind forwards again, to the army that slowed a few hundred feet from the final bend in the road.

They walked carefully now, losing their tight formation to spread over the road, some of them ducking into the trees.

An arrow pierced the neck of a mystic, and Julianne pounced, slashing through the first weakened shield she could find. This one controlled a guard, and an unwilling one at that. Despite the desperate craving for the mind-pleasure, he fought against it and ached to resist the presence in his mind.

Fight, she whispered to the trapped soul. *Run if you want, or fight with me.*

She left the guard, satisfied when a moment later, all hell broke loose. Still riding in the mind of a dazed mystic, she watched as one of the rear guards suddenly started thrashing, plowing through the tail end of the group with his weapon and laying waste to any who got in his way.

Two more arrows flew, meaty thwacks punctuating the cries of rage and pain. Then, two more. The army was in chaos, as mystics fell and their guards turned on them.

"Pair up, pair up!" The cry went out and bloodied hands reached out to form bonds.

One touched the hand of the mystic Julianne still held in thrall, and she let them begin the shielding process. Her partners gave her a mental shove, then screamed as their minds were engulfed in illusions.

Julianne showed them fiery arrows raining down, explosions and scorched, smoking bodies thrown into the air. One of them ran, the other sank to the ground screaming, arms over his head to protect him from the imaginary attack.

The hysteria spread as Julianne touched mind after mind, forcing her way through inadequate shields and infecting them with horror and despair.

Her knees buckled, and she pulled back. Exhaustion washed over her and she knew she'd come dangerously close to overdoing it. The sounds of battle clanged in her ears and even her meditation didn't dull them.

A hand grabbed hers, pulling Julianne away from the door.

"Come on, they're too close." Bastian wrapped an arm around her waist and half pulled, half lifted her towards the back of the house.

The front door slammed open and without hesitation, Bastian sent a magitech blast straight at the bearded man who filled the doorway. He was flung back onto the porch. Bastian kicked the door closed and threw the latch over it.

Moments later, footsteps thundered along the old wooden boards. "Come out, whore!" The rough voice sent chills down Julianne's spine.

She and Bastian ran along the back of the house. Fighting near the barn drowned out the voices that had joined the one in the house.

"Stop," Julianne snapped. "We don't run from this. We fight."

Bastian eyed her, then nodded. He lifted the weapon Marcus had given him and raised it. "Go that way. The dead tree near the barn is half rotted, hide inside it. You can see the house and the road from there."

Julianne grinned. "Where's the fun in that?"

When the first burly guard slammed Annie's back door open and stepped outside, Julianne waved. "Over here, ass maggot!"

"What the hell is an ass maggot?" Bastian hissed.

Julianne giggled as adrenaline filled her veins. "Something a friend taught me." She waited until the guard was halfway across the yard, then sprinted forwards. She thumped him on the head as she passed, twirling to a stop behind him. Another crack with her staff had him on the ground before he could strike at her once.

Two more people ran out of the house. "That one!" the first yelled, and two more joined them.

"This could be a little harder than expected," Julianne muttered. "Bastian, you take the orange one. Don't get hurt." She eyed the robed mystic. "You don't know what you're up against," she said.

Straightening from her fighting stance, Julianne whispered to herself as her eyes went white. She slammed into a solid shield. Instead of wasting valuable energy on it, she pulled back just enough to graze the minds of the guards, tightly wrapped in mental restraints.

"We're going to play it like this, are we?" Still in a trance, Julianne dropped her weight a little, balancing her staff in two hands. The attackers fanned out around her.

A guard moved in, and she thwacked him in the face with her staff, then ducked a punch from another. Her touch on their minds gave her the slightest edge as she read their intent before they moved.

"For guards, you guys are awfully bad at your job," she said as her stick crunched against one's fingers. He yelped and dropped his weapon, unable to move them even as his master dulled the pain. "That'll hurt later, I'm afraid."

"Finish her!" the mystic barked.

Three left. Julianne's head throbbed, and she squinted past the pain, unwilling to let her mind read drop even for an instant.

A guard stepped forward and she struck out, startled when she missed. Her mental control faltered and slipped away, leaving her deaf to his thoughts. The guard stood, trembling. Julianne darted a glance at his master and saw why immediately.

The mystics blue robes were wet and brown. Blood cascaded from his throat as he stared at her, eyes wide and mouth stammering silent words. He collapsed to the ground and behind him, a feral-eyed, bearded man palmed a bloodstained knife, then hobbled away on a thick walking stick. Long hair fell in dirty knots down his back.

"Who the hell was that?" Julianne muttered. Then, she remembered the guards. "Will you stay and fight?" she asked.

They exchanged glances. A moment later, all Julianne could see was their disappearing backs as they ran into the forest.

"Dammit," Julianne spat. A cry from the barn sent her running.

Bette and Garrett were faced off against each other. Bette scowled, carefully backing away while Garrett breathed hard, his small crossbow aimed at her. Sweat beaded on his forehead.

"Run, lass. Just run. I dinna think… I can't…"

"Fight it, Garrett!" Julianne couldn't even summon a flicker of her magic. "Bastian, find that mystic. I don't care if you have to throw rocks at their head."

Bastian nodded and ran off. Julianne stepped up next to Bette, hands up defensively. "Garrett, you can stop them. Just concentrate. Focus inside, find your core and slam it in their faces."

"Bullshit," Bette snapped. "That ass wipe couldn't fight off a brass balled monkey, let alone a mystic." Her eyes narrowed. "He couldn't even beat *me* in a real fight!"

Garrett screamed. He threw his arms wide, throwing the crossbow and roaring until his face went red and the veins in his neck looked ready to burst. "Like fuck I can't beat ye in a fight, rearick!" he yelled. A wide grin spread over his face. "But not today, Bette. Today, we fuck the mind fuckers."

Bette cheered and ran over to squeeze Garrett in a suffocating hug. She punched his arm, hard, and slapped his shoulder while laughing gleefully. "I knew ye'd fight the mind-fucking shit-stain off!" She didn't see the pained look on his face, and Julianne was too polite to mention it.

A shout rang out and the thud of a magitech blast trembled in the air. "Got him!" Bastian yelled from outside.

Together, the rearick ran through the barn entry, into the battle outside. Julianne slumped against a wall, closing her eyes and allowing herself a moment of meditation. The brief exercise didn't help her headache, but took some of the tiredness that sapped her power.

New faces had appeared in the battle outside. Julianne saw a toothless old man and a white-haired woman in the fray, along with children too young to be fighting.

Just as she wondered where they'd come from, she caught sight of foppish blonde hair bouncing through the guards as they fell. Marcus. *What the hell?*

Julianne took a steadying breath, then reached out to Bastian and Danil. *Time to light a fire under these bastards*, she sent. She slipped deeper into her meditation then, fortifying her strength as much as she could.

She worked an image, sending thin tendrils of smoke up from the nearby wood. It thickened, darkening the air even as flames began to lap the trees and grass. The army began to dissipate and some turned to run back down the road they'd marched on less than a hour before.

That's when it came. The big green beast rose from the trees on wings the size of wagons, its tail lashing angrily. He opened his maw and belched out a breath of burning flame. Julianne dropped her illusion and staggered back, raising her arms over her face as the creature turned its great head past her.

"Dragon!" The scream pierced the air and the last of the army fell, quivering in fear of the monstrous beast.

The townspeople cheered, weak voices sending out a frail cry that lifted her heart nonetheless.

"Hurry up, I can't hold this bloody thing all day."

Julianne spun. Behind her stood a grey-haired man, eyes white and face dirty. By his side, Marcus grinned.

She blinked. "Artemis?" she gasped.

"Yes?" He blinked back at her, waiting for a question.

"No, I mean…" Astounded, she looked towards the soldier instead. "Marcus, what the hell?"

Marcus chuckled. "Found him. Well, Annie did. I left her and Lilly in an old ruin. Her husband used to shelter there when he was on a hunt. Turns out old Artemis here had claimed the place as his own."

Artemis frowned. "No, I didn't. I was just living there. Never said it was mine."

Marcus gave him a sideways glance and nodded slowly. "Anyway, I thought I'd come back and see if I could help. Art wanted to see what was going on."

"Artemis," the old man grumped.

"Sorry. Artemis. Anyway, what are you going to do with all them? Surely you can't hold that dragon illusion up forever?" Marcus ran his eyes over the cowering army.

CHAPTER FORTY-ONE

"I still don't understand why you let them live," Marcus said. He gripped his empty cup, turning it in his hands.

Julianne plucked it out of his hands and set it firmly on the table. "Because we don't really know if they deserved to die," Julianne said. "Many of them were brainwashed into thinking they were serving a greater good. This leader of theirs really knows his stuff, I don't know how long it'll take to undo what he did. Or even if we can."

"It takes approximately three days to reverse the spell, then twelve more weeks for full rehabilitation," Artemis said, coming in. He dragged off his coat and looked for a place to put it. Not seeing anywhere good enough, he shrugged and dropped it on the floor.

"What do you know about it, mystic?" Marcus asked.

"I taught it to him. It wasn't hard. The shielding, too."

"To August?" Julianne struggled to put the pieces together in her mind.

"Don't be an idiot. August doesn't have a talented bone in his body. I taught Rogan, and he spread it to the rest once they were his. Or he tried to. Or maybe he didn't. The techniques these people used were crass and inefficient, though perhaps they have a more sustained effect. I really should look into that."

"Who's Rogan? And why the hell would you teach him how to control people like that?" Marcus picked his cup again, this time gripping it almost tight enough to crush the ceramic.

Julianne snatched it back. "Artemis, he's right. Rogan is Master of the Dawn, he's the leader of this damned cult. He's making people into slaves! You don't condone that, surely?"

Artemis gave an exasperated grunt. "I didn't *mean* to. I was researching. You can't study a spell without a subject. I didn't think he'd do… well, all that." He frowned, the long hairs of his brows drooping sadly. "He said he just wanted to be my friend. He probably didn't mean it. Most don't."

Julianne rubbed her head. "So, you can undo the spell that made them his lackeys? Free these mystics and the rest of the town?"

Artemis sat up. "The town? Oh no. They'll need more healing than a few weeks' worth. The mystics, though, he just used plain old magic on those. Feedback loop. Pretty simple when you think about it. I wonder why someone didn't come up with it before this."

"You'll help us, though?" Julianne asked, leaning over the table. "Help us undo the damage he caused?"

"Well, on account of it being my fault, I suppose I must." Artemis dug in his beard, scratching his chin. "Then what?"

Julianne fell silent, thinking it through. "We take in those who will help, rehabilitate the town. Once that's done, we can hunt down August—he wasn't among the dead, or those we captured—and try to find Rogan. And we deal with him—*permanently*."

"And the rest?" Marcus asked.

Julianne nodded gravely. "They have one chance. I hope that most of them acted outside of their own will, but any who didn't won't get the chance to do this to anyone else."

"Good, good. I'll teach you the trick of it, and how to link up for shielding, too. Designed that one myself, of course." Artemis nodded, eyes focused on something distant. "You do have them locked up, don't you?"

Julianne nodded. She, Bastian and Danil had locked the rogue mystics in the barn and sent Bette and Garrett to stay with Annie and Lilly until the problem was sorted. Until the spell was broken and the victims sorted from the perpetrators, Julianne didn't want anyone around who didn't have a rock-solid shield.

Reflexively, she checked Marcus. So far, his shields had held. One day, she'd get to the bottom of that. "Three days. You think you'll be ok that long, soldier?"

Marcus smiled. "As long as I have you by my side."

Julianne reached under the table and took his hand. "Three days. Then we start it all again. You sure you want to stick around for this?"

He winked. "Someone's gotta keep you outta trouble. Or help you get into it."

FINIS

Whew, what a whirlwind couple of months! I'm quickly scribbling these notes down in between tweaking some book two scenes and getting ahead on book three. I'm also checking in to my first appearance on the Facebook pages - you guys are all so sweet!

Putting work out is really nerve wracking, but the kind and supportive comments from the fans (who haven't read a thing I've written yet, mind you) have been amazing, so thank you.

Anyway, I guess you want to know a little about me. I'm an Aussie mum with three kids and a passion for writing and reading. Growing up, I was the 'weird kid' who walked around carrying books too big for my gangly arms and who could navigate the whole school without looking up from the pages my face was buried in.

Now my days are spent frantically scribbling words between bites of weetbix, cleaning up spills, breaking up fights and debating whether using mental magic to send naughty kids to bed would be unethical, if it were an option. It's hard - really hard, some days, but it's also the most fun I've ever had. To be able to create my own stories is a dream come true!

Speaking of dreams, this seems like a good time to drag Michael in. I remember when my first book came out. It wasn't doing great. I was a nobody in this huge group of writers that were making pots of money. I didn't feel like I had much to offer, but Michael still took the time to pull me in on a voice chat, making a space in his already packed schedule to offer advice and support to this fledgling writer.

I've never forgotten that first talk, or the way he offered so much of himself to so, so many people.

Fast forward a year and a bit, and my good friends Chris and Lee interviewed Michael on their podcast. Next thing I knew, they were jumping into the KGU and asking if I wanted to join them.

The Age of Magic channel in our Slack group (the program we use to talk, organize and track all the details that keep the worlds running) is like a close knit family. I knew good things about Brandon and had vaguely heard of PT and Candy before joining. Justin and I had spoken a bit before, so I knew I was in good company. I didn't expect it to be this much fun, though!

Anyway, I'll sign off now because I can get a bit rambley when I'm not following a scene by scene outline! And I know the consequence of wasting time when I could be writing more books.

I'll see you guys in a couple of days, when I write the notes for book two!

-Amy

First, THANK YOU for not only reading this book but reading all the way through to the Author Notes as well!

I only vaguely remember speaking with Amy (this would be over a year ago, I think) on that first video call. What I remember at the time (other than working to answer some questions) was "WOW, I'm speaking to an author that lives down under!"

It doesn't take much for me to feel impressed by speaking to others in foreign countries.

Later, I listened to the Part-Time Writers podcast with CM Raymond and LE Barbant (See it here: http://www.parttimewriters.com) and they mention Amy every few podcasts. Usually, because Amy was giving them some shit, and Chris is so willing to share all the stuff in their path to becoming full-time publishing authors.

Even the bad stuff Amy would tell them.

Somehow, these three became a trinity of friends giving each other a healthy dose of reality (which I secretly believe Chris thrives on. The worse the reality, the more he likes it.)

Amy speaks in her Author Notes about the guys having me on

their podcast, then poof they were writing in The Kurtherian Gambit.

I was on their podcast and challenged them to realize that from what I understood, they didn't know what their mountain (their goal) was with their stories. They firmly had one foot in the literature camp, and one foot in the fun-stories, pulp type genre.

They tried to do a mash-up, and it wasn't succeeding too well. Then, they were off on other trials and tribulations, but ALWAYS they were looking back, longingly, to their literature roots.

So, fast forward like a month. It's Christmas time 2016, and I get a request to chat from Chris - He's asking (because he is in the 20Booksto50k group and knew of some of the people I was collaborating with) if I was open to another collaboration?

Damn! What an honor to be asked.

We agreed to push the discussion until after Christmas, but that we were absolutely going to go forward, details to be figured out later.

Then, I hit them with a "What do you guys think about running the Age of Magic?" as we were working out the details... They accepted, and I was fist pumping -"WOOHOO!"

Fast forward a couple of months, and they said they had one particular author they wanted to bring with them...

Enter Amy Hopkins.

It was serendipitous that we all traveled in these circles, and that people that care for each other have the opportunity to help each other. We have processes to do our best when on boarding a new author and the guys have the responsibility to make sure we stay on track, pleasing the fans (JIT).

I had trust in them, they had trust in Amy, and now we have a new series and another author who is biting her fingernails hoping, no praying, that all of you like her books and characters... Or is she the one that is going to be the first to fail?

I don't think so, Amy - so you can stop biting your fingernails.

THANK YOU ALL for helping this self-professed nerd/geek

girl with scrawny arms, who would read books walking down the school hall to provide you with a few of her own stories…

Just like you did me, a little less than two years ago.

Ad Aeternitatem,
Michael

9 798888 788660